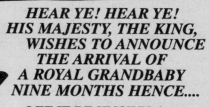

HEAR YE! HEAR YE!
HIS MAJESTY, THE KING,
WISHES TO ANNOUNCE
THE ARRIVAL OF
A ROYAL GRANDBABY
NINE MONTHS HENCE....

LET IT BE KNOWN that
Princess Alexandra, the King's
eldest daughter (and his once-
thought successor), is (rather
unexpectedly) expecting after a
sojourn to the United States....

LET IT ALSO BE KNOWN
that well-to-do Western rancher
(and self-appointed bodyguard)
Mitch Colton is father to the royal
baby on the way....

All of Wynborough celebrates the
proud parents-to-be—and eagerly
awaits further news of the
romance between the
princess and her cowboy.

Dear Reader,

Welcome to Special Edition...where each month we offer six wonderful new romances about people just like you—striving to find the perfect balance between life, career, family and, of course, love....

Those dynamic MONTANA MAVERICKS are back with brand-new stories to tell! Reader-favorite Christine Rimmer launches Special Edition's continuity, MONTANA MAVERICKS: RETURN TO WHITEHORN. In *Cinderella's Big Sky Groom*, a virginal beauty enters into a pretend engagement with the prince of her dreams. Then in December, the passion—and peril—continues in our 2-in-1 Special Edition book, *A Montana Mavericks Christmas*, featuring 2 brand-new novellas by Susan Mallery and Karen Hughes.

Also this November, look for *The No-Nonsense Nanny* by Penny Richards, about the trials and tribulations of a feisty nanny looking for a fresh start *and* a second chance with the town's sexy sheriff.

Silhouette's majestic five-book cross-line continuity, ROYALLY WED, begins with *A Royal Baby on the Way*. In this first installment by Susan Mallery, a headstrong princess searches for the missing crown prince...and finds herself in the family way! Follow the series next month in Silhouette Intimate Moments. And sparks fly in *Cowboy Boots and Glass Slippers* by Jodi O'Donnell when a modern-day Cinderella finally meets her match.

Rounding off the month, *Yours for Ninety Days* by Barbara McMahon is an evocative story about a mysterious loner who finds sweet solace with an enticing innocent. And an unlikely twosome find themselves altar-bound in *Pregnant & Practically Married* by Andrea Edwards— book three in the adorable THE BRIDAL CIRCLE miniseries.

Enjoy these unforgettable romances created *by* women like you, *for* women like you!

Sincerely,

Karen Taylor Richman
Senior Editor

Please address questions and book requests to:
Silhouette Reader Service
U.S.: 3010 Walden Ave., P.O. Box 1325, Buffalo, NY 14269
Canadian: P.O. Box 609, Fort Erie, Ont. L2A 5X3

SUSAN MALLERY

A ROYAL BABY ON THE WAY

SPECIAL EDITION®

Published by Silhouette Books
America's Publisher of Contemporary Romance

Special thanks and acknowledgment are given to Susan Mallery for her contribution to the Royally Wed series.

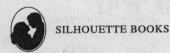 SILHOUETTE BOOKS

ISBN 0-373-24281-6

A ROYAL BABY ON THE WAY

Visit us at www.romance.net

Printed in U.S.A.

SUSAN MALLERY

lives in sunny Southern California where the eccentricities of a writer are considered fairly normal. Her books are both reader favorites and bestsellers, with recent titles appearing on the Waldenbooks bestseller list and the *USA Today* bestseller list. Her 1995 Special Edition novel, *Marriage on Demand*, was awarded Best Special Edition by *Romantic Times Magazine*.

THE WYNDHAMS

Prince Phillip Wyndham (King of Wynborough)

m.

Gabriella Clark (Queen of Wynborough)

James (presumed dead)	**ALEXANDRA** m. **MITCH COLTON**	Elizabeth	Katherine	Serena
MAN... MERCENARY... MONARCH *Special Edition* on sale February 2000	A ROYAL BABY ON THE WAY *Special Edition #1281* on sale October 1999	THE PREGNANT PRINCESS *Desire* on sale January 2000	UNDERCOVER PRINCESS *Intimate Moments #968* on sale November 1999	THE PRINCESS'S WHITE KNIGHT *Silhouette Romance #1415* on sale December 2000

Prologue

"Alex, I think you should take a look at this."

Princess Alexandra Wyndham, the oldest of King Phillip's four daughters, glanced up from the computer printout she'd been scanning. It was nearly eleven in the morning and she was, as usual, buried in her daily reports. The kingdom of Wynborough might not be huge, but it required a large staff to keep things running smoothly. Despite the efficiency of the palace's employees and loyalty of the senior staff, Alex insisted on overseeing many things herself. She spent her mornings in her office, looking for potential problems and smoothing them out before anyone noticed they'd been there in the first place. Her afternoons and evenings were reserved for state functions and occasionally, very occasionally, time for herself.

Alex set down the papers and smiled at Laura

Bishop, the social secretary who had been with the royal family for five years. "Another marriage proposal from an American rock star?" Alex asked. "While I don't understand them, I do confess to being flattered. After all, I'll be thirty next year. Not exactly the right age to be a bimbo." She wrinkled her nose. "Is that term still in use or am I being old-fashioned again?"

Laura grinned. "I think bimbo still works, although it's not really appropriate when used to describe a princess." Her smile faded. "No marriage proposal this time. It's a little more serious than that. I didn't know what to do with this." She waved the single sheet of paper. "I thought about going to the king, but he and your mother are busy with plans for the celebration and I wasn't sure...." Her voice trailed off.

Alex gave Laura her full attention. The royal social secretary was many wonderful things, including efficient. It wasn't like her to be indecisive about anything.

"All right," Alex said slowly and held out her hand. When Laura gave her the letter, she scanned it quickly, then read it a second time. Her breath caught in her throat and her chest tightened. "Dear Lord, can this be right?"

"I don't know," Laura admitted.

Was it possible? Alex shook her head to clear it, but her confused thoughts refused to be put in order. What to do?

"I'm glad you didn't go to my parents," Alex said slowly. "If it's true, then it's wonderful news, but if it isn't, they could be devastated all over again. I don't want that.''

Laura nodded. ''That's what I thought, too. I don't know the whole story, but I've read about the basics.''

''I don't think anyone knows the whole story. That's part of the problem.'' She set the letter on her desk. ''All right. Tell my sisters that I need to see them immediately.'' She glanced at her slender, elegant gold watch. ''Have them meet me for lunch in our private dining room at noon. I'll tell the kitchen to have something simple sent up.'' She looked at her friend. ''I'll want you to be there, too, Laura.''

Laura stared back at her. ''Are you sure? Isn't this a family matter?''

''Yes, but I suspect we're going to need your help. I have a couple of ideas. If my sisters agree with my plan, then you'll be an important part of things.'' Despite her shock, Alex managed a smile. ''As usual.''

''Thank you.''

After Laura left, Alex turned in her chair and stared out the window. The view was nearly as familiar as her own reflection. She'd spent many hours in this office, working, planning and, during rare moments of quiet, dreaming. While Wyndham Castle was a major tourist attraction, and even now a large group of visitors toured the manicured gardens below her third-story window, it was also her home. She'd been born here, grown up, played, laughed and cried, all within the confines of the old stone-and-wood structure. People she met often asked her what it was like to live in a castle, but for Alexandra it was all she'd ever known. If she occasionally wondered what it would be like to live a normal life, she reminded herself that she'd been blessed by her circumstances and her loving family. She had wonderful parents and three sisters with whom she was very close.

Without turning around, she reached behind her and picked up the letter Laura had brought her. As she fingered the inexpensive writing paper, she considered how she'd thought her future was set. Was that all about to change?

"We should go skiing over the holidays," Serena said as she scooped some chicken and mango salad onto her plate. She picked up a piece of mango and popped it in her mouth. Impish lights danced in her green eyes. "There are always so many good-looking men at the chalets and goodness knows you three all need to get married before you're over the hill."

Alex looked at her baby sister and tried not to take the comment personally. As the oldest, she *should* be married first, and no doubt her parents would get around to arranging a match in the near future. But right now that was not her most pressing issue.

"We have something more important to discuss," Alex said as she glanced around the table.

A lace antique cloth protected the gleaming oval surface. Water, iced tea and soft drinks had been poured into crystal goblets. Alex sat at the head of the table with Serena and Laura to her left and Katherine and Elizabeth to her right.

"You look serious," Katherine said. "Is something wrong?"

"Not exactly." Alex paused as she tried to figure

out how best to share the news. "Laura opened a letter this morning and immediately brought it to me. I made the decision not to share the contents with our parents. They're both busy with the business of running the kingdom, not to mention the celebration of Father's twentieth year as monarch."

"We know all this," Serena said and rolled her eyes. "Alex, you could make a roller-coaster ride boring if you tried. What has you all in a huff? What's in the letter?"

Alex glanced at her other two sisters and saw them nod. She chose to believe they were encouraging her to read them the message and not agreeing with Serena's assessment of her personality.

She pulled the single sheet of paper out of her jacket pocket and cleared her throat.

"Dear Royal Family. I saw something on the news today about your king celebrating his kingship of your country. While I didn't find this especially interesting, I happened to see a picture of the family crest—is that what it's called? That shield with the thingamajigs? Anyway, seeing that reminded me of something that happened a long time ago."

Alex heard a catch of breath. She glanced up and saw all three of her sisters staring at her.

"Nearly thirty years ago I was housekeeper for a place called The Sunshine Home for Children in Hope, Arizona. One day I noticed a real fine piece of linen in the laundry. It was some kind of blanket and I decided to take it for my own use. I knew it belonged to one of the children, but I didn't think they would miss it. It was the nicest tea cozy I'd ever had and now I realize it had your crest on it. With all this fuss about the celebration and all, there have also been stories about your lost boy, James. It got me to thinking. Three boys came to The Sunshine Home that year around the time of the kidnapping. They were all the right age to be your boy. One of them could belong to your family. My memory's not what it used to be and I can't remember all of them, but I do sure recall John Colton. He was a real scrapper. I'm not saying John's the one, but I'll bet my last pair of boots that he would know where to find the others.''

Alex put down the letter. ''She signs it 'Most Sincerely, Grandma Beulah Whitaker.' Oh, and she would like a picture of the four princesses sent to her if we have time.''

There was a moment of silence, then everyone started talking at once. It had taken Alex a few minutes to gather her own composure after absorbing the news, so she understood her sisters' confusion and questions.

''Do you think it's really possible that James is alive?'' Katherine asked.

Elizabeth shook her head. ''It's been what, twenty-nine years? Could he have survived all that time and we never knew?''

"Let's go to America and find him," Serena said with a broad grin. "I'll go. I can be ready to leave this afternoon."

Alex glared at her baby sister. There was no way she would trust that wild young woman alone in a foreign land. Given Serena's determination to find romantic adventure, she would forget about looking for James and set about getting herself in trouble as quickly as possible.

"First things first," Alex said calmly. "Do you all agree with my decision to keep this from our parents? I don't want to get their hopes up only to dash them again, but I would like to hear what you three think."

Katherine leaned toward her. Her gray eyes darkened with sadness. "None of us was born when they lost James, but I can imagine their pain. Mother hasn't spoken about it much, but when she does mention those days after James was kidnapped, she always cries. They have both worked very hard to bring prosperity to Wynborough. As they prepare for the twentieth anniversary of Father's coronation next year, they should be happy. Telling them about this letter will only distract them."

Elizabeth, normally a close and loving confidant for Alex, looked distracted. In the past couple of months, things had changed for the sister closest to her in age. Unfortunately Alex hadn't figured out what, and Elizabeth resisted all her gentle questions.

Elizabeth focused on the issue at hand long enough to nod her agreement. "Katherine's right. I don't think either of them want to go through that pain again. We should investigate this ourselves."

Alex glanced at Laura. Her social secretary raised her hands. "I'm just the hired help. I'd prefer not to vote."

"You're more than that," Serena said, giving Laura a quick hug. "You're practically one of the family." She grinned at Alex. "I say we find him ourselves and present him as a gift to Mother and Father. Their lost son returns home after twenty-nine years. Everyone will be so thrilled that there's finally an heir."

Alex stiffened slightly at the words, then tried not to notice as everyone's attention shifted to her. She knew what her sisters were thinking. That as the oldest, she'd taken on most of the responsibilities of heir. She worked hard and frequently traveled abroad to represent her country. But Wynborough law stated that the heir must be a son. While there had been some discussion about parliament changing the law, to date nothing had been done. After all, King Phillip was still in the prime of his life. There was no concern about the monarchy. But it left Alex in the awkward position of being a potential heir-in-waiting without knowing if that was going to happen.

That's not important, she told herself, and firmly pushed those thoughts away. Right now she and her sisters had to concentrate on their brother. If James was still alive, how were they to find him?

"Obviously we have to go to America," Alex said. "That's where the kidnapping occurred."

"I could arrange a publicity tour," Laura said. "There has been talk of bringing worldwide attention to King Phillip's years as a successful monarch. If all four of you were willing to travel to the States, you could quietly inquire about your brother while promoting Wynborough and the king.''

"Of course we'll go," Serena said. "At least *I* will.''

"No one's in doubt about that," Alex said dryly. She glanced at Katherine and Elizabeth. "Is this all right with you two?''

They both nodded. "I could use a change of scenery," Elizabeth said.

Again Alex wondered what had happened to make her sister so quiet these days. But if Elizabeth didn't want to talk, nothing was going to make her.

Alex opened the file next to her plate. "I think the best plan would be to start the investigation at the scene of the crime. James was kidnapped from the family home in Aspen, Colorado. While the place hasn't been used in years, I checked and it has been maintained by caretakers. They could have it ready for us in two days—so that will be our base of operation. Laura will put together a publicity schedule that leaves us plenty of time to search. In fact, I intend to go to Arizona to talk with 'Grandma Beulah' as soon as we arrive in the States.''

Katherine leaned forward. Like all the sisters, her hair was a variation on the theme of red. She had thick chestnut hair and wide gray eyes. Sensible as always, she asked, "How on earth are we going to get our parents to agree to this? They've never wanted us to visit America before. Do you really think they'll let all four of us go there?''

"Let me handle that," Alex said. "Laura and I will

come up with something. You just get ready to leave.''

Serena bounced to her feet. "I'm going to Disneyland."

"Not if any of us can help it," Elizabeth murmured under her breath as she stood up.

"Okay, then New York or California or Las Vegas."

Alex drew in a deep breath and told herself to remain calm. Serena was a handful and she was going to require around-the-clock watching. "Make a note," she told Laura as they left the small dining room. "Put extra security on Serena."

"Gabriel Morgan's our man," Laura said. "Plus, he's American, so he'll be most at home."

"Good. The last thing we need is a wild princess on the loose."

"What about Elizabeth and Katherine? Or for that matter, you?"

Alex laughed. "As if anything would ever happen to us. I promise you that except for possibly finding our long-lost brother, nothing exciting is going to happen while we're in America."

Chapter One

Mitch Colton could smell trouble a mile away...or right in his own driveway. Especially when it came packaged in a sleek, midnight-blue Jaguar. He'd been on his way into the house after spending the morning in the barn with a sick cow when the sound of a car engine had caught his attention. And not just any car engine, but one belonging to an elegantly beautiful sports car.

He stared as the vehicle came to a stop in front of the wide porch that encircled the low, one-story ranch house. While he could admire the sleek lines of the car, he didn't get the point. Sure, he could buy one, or even a dozen if he was so inclined, but he lived on a working ranch, and a car like that wasn't practical.

Neither was the leggy redhead stepping out from behind the wheel.

Mitch blinked. Redhead? As in a woman? He looked closer. Yup, and to quote his father, she was a looker. Well dressed in a toast-colored sweater dress, the hem of which flirted with her calves. She was slender, with plenty on top to capture any man's interest. Sunglasses hid her eyes, but enough of her face showed to convince him that she was somewhere between very pretty and knock-out gorgeous. Long, auburn curls fell down her back. Not bad for a Sunday afternoon, he thought.

"Good afternoon," the woman said as she approached the porch. "Are you Mitch Colton?"

He frowned. She sounded funny. Almost English, but not quite. She sure as hell wasn't from around here. He pushed his hat farther back on his head, propped one foot on the porch railing, leaned forward and rested his forearms on his raised thigh.

"That depends on who's doing the asking."

He'd half expected her to get annoyed, but she surprised him by smiling. "Don't you sound like the local sheriff in a Western movie. All right, cowboy, we'll do this your way." She pulled off her sunglasses, extended her hand and approached the porch. "I'm Alex Wyndham. If you are Mitch Colton, I'm very pleased to make your acquaintance."

He'd been holding his own, right up until she smiled and removed her sunglasses. The one-two punch of full lips curving in delight and baby-blue eyes hit him like whisky on an empty stomach. He straightened, swore silently, then leaned down to take her fingers in his. Even though he braced for the impact, the not-so-unexpected jolt of awareness crackled down to his toes. On the return trip, it settled somewhere a tad more interesting. Geez. All this over one little smile. Imagine what would happen to his body if she laughed, or God forbid, made that throaty purring sound women were so good at when they wanted a man.

He straightened and cleared his throat. "Ma'am."

Her smile broadened. "Ma'am. I'm sure you're using that mode of address for different reasons than is normally the case. But I like it."

Okay, now he was officially lost. "What are you talking about?"

"Nothing. I'm just savoring the moment. Here I am having a real conversation with a real cowboy. You are a cowboy, aren't you?"

"Yeah." He drew the single syllable out a couple of beats, then sighed. He didn't like the new direction of their conversation. "You're not some buckle bunny out looking for a ride, are you? I didn't do that kind of thing when I was a kid, and I'm sure as hell not going to do it now."

Her delicate eyebrows pulled together in a frown. She had the most perfect skin he'd ever seen. Except maybe on a baby's butt. Faint color stained her cheeks, but he would have bet a prime steer or two that it was natural, not out of a compact. Her eyes were large, her lashes dark. High cheekbones and a pointed chin focused attention on her full mouth. Dress her up in some leather and lace and she would look like the poster girl for sin.

"Buckle bunny?" His guest shook her head. "Are you talking about a rabbit? Don't you have cattle on this ranch? I didn't know anyone bred rabbits out West. Is there a market for them?"

"What are you talking about?" he asked. Rabbits? Was she crazy?

"Rabbits. You mentioned them. Well, you actually said bunnies, but aren't they the same thing? Are we having trouble communicating?"

"One of us is." He folded his arms over his chest and glared down at her. Was she being dumb on purpose? "Why don't you tell me why you're here, lady."

She flashed him another smile. "Actually, I'm looking for your brother. John Colton. Could you tell me where he is?"

While her conversation about rabbits had done a whole bunch to dilute his desire, her question squashed the last, lingering flicker of interest. Over the years he'd come to terms with his relationship with his brother, but he refused to be attracted to one of John's old lovers.

He raked his gaze over her, starting at her expensive boots and ending at the riot of curls on the top of her head. "First of all, I don't give out personal information to strangers. Second, you don't look like his type."

"Type?"

The woman stared at him blankly. She repeated the word again, silently, as if trying to figure out what he meant. Her surprise was so genuine, he had to reassess his opinion of her.

"You think we were involved?" she asked, faintly bewildered. "Oh, my. No, it's not that at all."

But before she could explain exactly what their relationship was, or he could ask, a black sedan pulled into his yard and parked behind the Jag. Must be his day for company, he thought as two men in dark suits stepped out of the car.

Mitch might have spent most of his life either on the ranch or the rodeo circuit, but he knew security people when he saw them. The not-so-subtle bulges under their left arms came from handguns, not muscles.

"You've got my attention now, lady," he said.

"Alex," she murmured as she turned to look at the two strangers. "Just plain Alex."

He ignored her statement, mostly because it didn't make sense. Interestingly enough, the two thugs were ignoring him, too. What was going on?

"Why don't you tell me who you are and what the hell you're doing here?" Mitch asked.

One of the security men looked up and nodded politely, then spoke to the woman. "Princess Alexandra, you know you're not allowed to go off unescorted. You've only been in this country a short time and you're not familiar with the driving laws, nor will you know how to communicate with the local citizens."

"They're just people, Rowan. I've been communicating just fine." The woman laughed.

How nice that she was amused, Mitch thought. Then he replayed the man's statement a couple of dozen times in his brain. Princess Alexandra? Had he really said *Princess?*

"No way," he muttered, mostly to himself. "Not a real princess."

Alex, or Princess Alexandra or whomever she was, turned to face him and shrugged. "Sorry, yes. I'm a real princess. I have a king and queen for parents, three princesses for sisters. There's even a palace."

His mind went blank. All he could do was stand there and repeat the same thing over and over again. "A princess? A real princess?" She didn't look like a princess, he thought, staring at her dress and then her face. There wasn't any crown or whatever it was princesses wore. "This is a joke, right?"

"I'm afraid not." Her gaze moved to the two security men standing next to her. "He doesn't seem to be understanding me. Maybe you're right. Maybe I will have some trouble communicating."

That comment got through to Mitch. It also annoyed him. "I'm not stupid," he said. "I heard what you said, I just don't believe it."

The woman nodded slightly. "I suppose in your position I would feel the same way." She motioned to the house. "Would it be possible to go inside and talk about this?"

He looked at the two armed men. To think the most excitement he'd been expecting in his quiet Sunday afternoon had been to catch a couple of football games on television. "Sure. Will the rent-a-cops let you do that?"

Neither security person responded to his mild insult. The taller of the two turned to the woman. "We're going to have to search the house."

"Do you mind?" Alex asked Mitch. "It's really a formality. I'm sure you're very safe."

"Thanks for the vote of confidence." He had the strangest feeling that he'd been dropped into a movie somewhere in the middle. He had no clue what was going on and he wasn't sure he wanted to know.

"If you'll give me a minute," the taller man said, then walked up the three stairs and across the porch. He paused at the front door.

"You're kidding, right?" Mitch asked.

"Not really."

The bodyguard slipped a thin wallet out of his jacket pocket...the one on the opposite side from the gun. He opened it and handed it to Mitch.

Mitch studied the official badges. The top one showed a royal coat of arms, while the bottom came from the U.S. State Department.

"There's a photo ID as well," the man offered helpfully.

Mitch flipped to the picture and noted the card below, then handed the wallet back to Reginald Rowan, security expert and a man licensed to carry a handgun in at least two countries.

"Door's open," Mitch said. "I don't bother much with locks. There aren't many strangers out here. At least not until today."

"How nice," Alex said as she glanced around. "It's very private. You must like that."

"I guess."

His gaze moved from her back to the remaining security agent, to the bulge of the man's gun, to the sleek Jag parked in front of the house. If it was a joke, someone had gone to a lot of trouble to make it look real. He shrugged. What did it matter? He would play along for a while, just to figure out what everyone wanted.

Twenty minutes later he and Alex, as she'd insisted he call her despite frowns of annoyance from the security men, sat across from each other at the old oak table in the kitchen. Mitch tried to concentrate on what his guest was saying, but all he could think was how ticked off Betty, his housekeeper, was going to be if Alex turned out to be the real thing and she'd missed her chance to meet royalty.

"So the last time my parents were in America was twenty-nine years ago," Alex said, continuing her story. "They brought their child, James, with them. He was barely a year old."

"And that's when he was kidnapped?" Mitch asked.

"Right. They'd been staying at the family home in Aspen, Colorado. I don't know all the details, of course. I wasn't even born. From what I've learned, a massive search was instigated, but it was as if the baby had just disappeared. A ransom note had been received, confirming everyone's belief that the kidnapping was for monetary gain and not political purposes."

"But your family didn't pay in time?"

Alex leaned forward and rested her forearms on the scarred table. "That part is a little hazy. I think the ransom was collected, but before it could be delivered, the authorities found the kidnapper's hideout.

Through some freak accident, the small cabin burned to the ground during the rescue attempt. The kidnapper's body was found and identified, and a few bits of my brother's clothing were discovered. He was presumed dead. Only recently did I receive this letter.''

She pulled a single sheet of paper from her handbag and passed it to him. Mitch read it once, quickly, then a second time. He was having trouble keeping track of everything going on. One minute he'd been admiring a pair of pretty legs and the next he was reading about a lost royal heir.

He glanced up from the sheet. ''This could be a hoax.''

''I know, but we have to assume it's not. What if my brother really is still alive?''

''So that's why you want to talk to John.''

She nodded. ''We have no way of knowing if he's James or not. According to Grandma Beulah, whom I spoke with yesterday, she thinks it's one of the other two.'' Alex pressed her full lips together. ''I don't know what to tell you about her information. She's a lovely woman, but her memory has faded and I wasn't completely convinced she even knew why I was visiting her. From what I can piece together, three boys around the same age came to The Sunshine Home within a short time of the kidnapping. That information, combined with the fact that a baby's body was never recovered at the fire and Grandma Beulah's possession of James's baby blanket means there's a possibility my brother is still alive.'' Her blue eyes darkened. "I don't suppose you remember anything that might be helpful."

"I was four when my family adopted John. Sorry, but I don't remember much except being annoyed at having to share my toys."

She sighed. "I understand. I'm not sure why I'm surprised that this is proving difficult. I suppose I had hoped my sisters and I would fly over here and just figure out what had happened. An unrealistic expectation on my part. The trail is years old, and the odds of James being alive have to be slim. But we're determined to learn as much as we can."

"Why did your parents send you instead of hiring a private investigator?"

Alex flushed slightly. "The king and queen don't know about the letter. There have been so many false leads over the years. None of us wanted to upset them again, especially with them preparing for the celebration."

Every time he thought he'd figured out what was going on, she threw him another curve. "What celebration?"

"My father will have been king for twenty years next year. The entire country will be honoring him. It's a time of great joy, and my sisters and I didn't want to distract my parents from that. If we do find James, then their happiness will be complete. If not, they won't have to deal with any more disappointment."

She folded her hands primly together. Mitch noticed she hadn't touched the mug of coffee he'd offered her. Wasn't it up to royal standards? Uh-oh. If he was worrying about royal standards, that meant he believed her story. Which meant he believed that she was a princess. Maybe he'd been kicked in the head earlier that day and hadn't noticed.

"As far as our parents are concerned," Alex continued, "we're on a tour of your country, publicizing the upcoming celebration. We're making several public appearances. The investigation is being kept quiet."

Mitch half glanced over his shoulder. Was there going to be more of an invasion? "Where are your sisters now?"

"In Aspen. I'm here to talk to John and to go through records at The Sunshine Home. Laura, our social secretary, is setting that up with the present administration."

If Alex wasn't a real princess, she sure had her act together. She spoke formally enough to be royalty. Her accent intrigued him. As did her perfect posture and the faint tilt of her head. He thought about asking if she had any ID with her—maybe a business card with a little crown on it or something.

He held back a grin. This wasn't really happening, he thought. Women like her didn't stroll into the lives of men like him. He was a decent guy with a successful ranch. He'd been told he was good-looking, and for what it was worth he believed it. But a princess? No way.

"When is he coming back?" Alex asked, interrupting his train of thought.

Mitch looked at her. "Who? John?"

She nodded. "Will he be home this evening?"

Mitch took a long swallow of coffee. "I don't know when John will come home. He's not gone for the day, he's just gone. He does that kind of thing. He takes off without saying anything and comes back when he's done with whatever he'd been doing."

Alex stiffened. "What are you saying? Where does he go?"

"Hell if I know. He doesn't talk about it. It's just his way. He's been doing it since he was a teenager. For a while my folks tried to keep him on the ranch, but he refused. He was too big to send to his room, so they let him go." What he wasn't going to tell her was that for a long time he'd been happy to see his brother leave. In the past couple of years, though, he'd come to terms with many things and now he missed John when he was gone.

"But what if you have to get in touch with him? He must phone."

"Sometimes. Not always." His gaze narrowed. "I don't know what the rules are like where you come from, but here in this country, no one has to check in if he doesn't want to."

Her full lips pursed in obvious annoyance. "I assure you that Wynborough is not a dictatorship. My point was simply that family members often prefer to stay in touch. What if there was an emergency with your parents?"

"I don't have an answer to that. I guess John would just have to live with what happened."

Her shoulders slumped a little, the first slip of otherwise perfect posture. "But I have to talk with him."

"You really think he might be your brother?"

Mitch asked doubtfully. John, the lost royal prince? Mitch turned the idea over in his mind. No, it wasn't possible, was it?

"I don't know what to think," Alex admitted. "I just know that I must speak with him."

They both heard footsteps from the hallway. The security men walked into the kitchen. "Princess Alexandra, how long are you planning to stay this afternoon?" the taller of the two asked. "We have a long drive ahead of us."

Alex looked at Mitch. "Could it really be weeks until he comes back?"

Mitch nodded.

She drew in a breath. "Mr. Colton has informed me that his brother is away for an unspecified period of time that could turn into several weeks. I intend to stay in the area until he returns."

"That's not possible," the security agent told her. "We can't spare the manpower to keep you safe here and to watch your sisters."

"Then hire more people."

"And alert your parents?"

"You're right," Alex said slowly. "They would question additional security personnel, and I don't want them worrying."

"Return to Aspen. You can ask Mr. Colton to phone you when his brother returns."

Alex rose to her feet. She was tall, five-nine or five-ten. There was something regal about her bearing, and when she turned her full attention on the security agent, Mitch almost felt sorry for the man.

"I'm going to assume that was a suggestion and

not an order, Rowan,'' she said, her voice crackling with ice.

The man inclined his head briefly. ''Yes, Your Highness. However, it *is* my responsibility to keep you and your sisters safe. That means keeping you together.''

''We have plans to go to different parts of the country as part of our tour. We'll be attending various social functions.''

''Agreed, and we have security set up for all those venues. What we don't have is enough manpower to set up a separate home base here in a hotel. You would be at risk, and I will not allow that, ma'am.''

It was a battle of wills, Mitch thought as he leaned back, bracing his chair on two legs. Given the odds, he would put all his money on the princess. She didn't look like the kind of woman who gave in easily.

''I'm not leaving,'' she said evenly. ''I want to be close so that I can speak to John Colton as soon as he returns. I also need to spend some time going through records at The Sunshine Home. I can do neither of those things from Aspen.'' She raised her hand to silence the other man before he could interrupt. ''If you want me to live somewhere secure, I will. I know a place that is relatively isolated and has already passed a security check.'' She turned to Mitch. ''Would it be too much trouble if I stayed here with you until your brother returned?''

Chapter Two

Mitch's mouth dropped open at the same time his chair thumped down onto all four legs. Based on the stunned expression on his face, Alex realized she'd caught him off guard with her question. She didn't want to turn around and look at either of her security people. Rowan, the one in charge of her personal safety, would get coldly quiet, and his assistant, Ted, would be gaping like a fish. She decided to plunge ahead before any of the men could start with the protests.

"It would only be for a short time," Alex said quickly, focusing all her attention on Mitch. "I would only need a place to sleep and somewhere to set up a small office. I know this would be a tremendous imposition, but I desperately need to speak with your brother. If he's not the missing heir, then he might know something important about the others. I'll be happy to pay whatever you'd like.''

At her final statement, Mitch's shocked expression shifted to narrow-eyed irritation. ''This isn't about money,'' he said slowly.

Too late Alex realized she'd offended her potential host. ''Yes, of course. I didn't mean—''

But she never got to say what she didn't mean. Rowan was already talking.

''This is completely out of the question, ma'am. I cannot spare the personnel necessary to keep you safe here on a ranch in the middle of Arizona. You must return to Aspen and stay with your sisters.''

Rowan's gaze also narrowed. What was it with men and their steely looks? She braced herself, knowing that the by-the-book bodyguard was about to play his trump card. ''If I don't receive your cooperation in this matter, I will be forced to go to the king.''

Alex felt herself being maneuvered into a corner. If Rowan called her father, there was no way she could keep their mission in America a secret. She had to keep the security agent's cooperation *and* stay on the ranch. Talking to John Colton was important.

''I'm not sure I see the problem,'' Alex said with a calm she didn't feel. ''The ranch is isolated, which works to our advantage. Who would look for me here?''

Rowan stepped closer to her. He lowered his voice. ''You don't know what you're talking about. This is a matter best left to professionals. While Mr. Colton passed the preliminary background check we did yesterday, there is no telling what a more detailed study might find. What do you know about him or the people who work here?''

"Wait one damn minute," Mitch said, coming to his feet. "I'll vouch for every cowboy on this ranch. Just because we don't live in some fancy castle doesn't mean we're not decent, hardworking folks.''

"I'm sure that's true," Rowan said with obvious insincerity, "however it does nothing to ensure the princess's personal safety.''

Alex had to press her lips together to keep from smiling. If Rowan and Mitch were going to get into a male power contest, then she was bound to win. The harder Rowan pushed, the more Mitch would shove back. In a matter of minutes the cowboy would be insisting she stay for as long as she liked.

"My family has been safe enough here for three generations," Mitch growled.

"Your family hardly compares to a royal princess.''

"So you're saying we're not good enough for the likes of her.''

Rowan clearly saw his mistake a moment too late. "Not at all," he amended. "It's more a matter of not knowing enough about you.''

Mitch took a step toward him. The cowboy was about three inches taller and twenty pounds heavier. From what Alex could tell, every one of those pounds was muscle. Mitch had shoulders broad enough to, well, be an old-time movie cowboy, she thought as she studied the way he went toe-to-toe with Rowan. His hair was a medium brown, a few shades lighter than Rowan's. It was also a bit longer, just grazing the collar of his blue work shirt. The contrast between the two men's dress—Rowan in his tailored suit and Mitch in jeans and boots—highlighted the differences in their personalities. Rowan was content to work for the royal family, keeping their princesses safe. Alex suspected Mitch had never worked for anyone but himself and that he preferred it that way.

"Maybe you should take a few more minutes to find out about me," Mitch said.

"This situation is out of the question."

Mitch jerked a thumb at Alex. "Seems to me the lady is the one in charge. Now why don't you go do what you have to so she can get her way in this?"

Alex's mouth twitched again, but she forced herself to maintain a pleasantly neutral, faintly regal expression. It was one she'd perfected in her teens, after hours of practicing in front of a mirror. When Rowan pulled a cellular phone from his pocket and ventured out of the kitchen, Mitch gave her a quick wink.

He was nice, she thought with some surprise. She'd been so caught up in the excitement of actually being on a working ranch, then disappointed that John Colton wasn't available, that she hadn't paid much attention to her host. He had an ease about him. Even though he was having a little trouble dealing with the fact that she was a princess, he didn't let the information overwhelm him. She had a feeling he was one of those people who would quickly forget the fact and start treating her like a regular person. The thought was heady indeed. She was rarely allowed to be anything but the eldest daughter of a king.

"Is this really that important?" Mitch asked. "I

don't usually get into power struggles with complete strangers, but I didn't like his attitude.''

Rowan and Ted had retired to one of the other rooms. She could hear both of their voices as they made the necessary calls to find out all they could about Mitch Colton and his ranch.

''It's important to my family,'' she said. It was also important to her, but she wasn't going to share her personal reasons for wanting to know the truth about her brother. She couldn't say she missed James. She'd been born nearly a year after he'd been kidnapped so they'd never met. But until she knew for sure if there was a male heir to the Wynborough throne, she couldn't plan her life.

''Seems like a lot of fuss just to have a conversation,'' Mitch told her. His gaze moved down her body, then retraced the journey back to her face. ''You look like the kind of woman who makes trouble. That true?''

This time Alex allowed herself to smile. ''I don't believe I've ever made trouble in the past.''

''Right.'' The single word was issued in a tone of disbelief. ''In my experience, someone as attractive as you can't help but make trouble.''

Alex felt a flush of pleasure stain her cheeks. He thought she was attractive? ''Thank you.''

''You can take it as a compliment if you want, but I didn't mean it in a good way. I don't want trouble in my life. I like things just the way they are.''

''I'm not going to change things.''

He shook his head. ''You can't help it, princess. You've got high maintenance written all over you.''

Alex was reasonably confident she'd been insulted, but she wasn't sure how. "High maintenance? What does that mean?"

He walked to the large window over the sink and stared out at the well-tended yard beyond. It was late October and many of the flowers had lost their blossoms, but lush green stalks still grew up toward the sun.

"It means you've got more luggage than what's in your trunk and that I'm going to regret not letting your security guy win."

She stiffened. "While I do have more luggage that will be sent to me, I promise not to get in the way. I'll need a bedroom and some place to set up an office. I have to stay in touch with both my sisters and the palace." She thought about the logistics. "Maybe a couple of phone lines for calls and the fax machine. The computer can share that line and…" She glanced at him. "Is that what you meant by high maintenance? I assure you I will cover any expenses."

"I don't doubt that for a minute." He jerked his head toward the closed kitchen door. "Your security people are going to give me and my employees the all clear, so let me give you the nickel tour and you can start planning your redecorating."

As he left the bright kitchen, Alex trailed after him. "Mr. Colton, I sense your resistance to this plan. While I need to be close to speak with your brother when he returns, I won't stay here if you find the idea repugnant."

He'd walked into a large living room. Like the kitchen, the room was big with hardwood floors and oversize pieces of furniture. Brightly colored rugs picked up tones from the sofas and the paintings on the walls. A huge rock fireplace dominated the far wall. It was a room one could relax in, she thought as her gaze drifted from the dozens of family pictures over the mantel to the handmade afghan over the back of the sofa.

Mitch stopped in the middle of the room and spun on his heel to face her. "Let's get a couple of things straight. First, call me Mitch. I'll call you Alex, even if it's gonna give your security people a seizure."

"Rowan's more of a silent suffering kind of individual."

Mitch's stern expression relaxed a little. He had warm brown eyes, she thought. And a very nice mouth—well shaped and firm looking, without being hard. She'd never really taken the time to notice a man's mouth before. How strange that she should do so now.

"Second," Mitch went on, "try to avoid using really big words. It's not that I don't have a college degree, but folks around here prefer life simple and their friends straightforward. You're a little fancy for the ranch, so you're going to have a work at fitting in."

Alex didn't know how to respond to that. "I'll do my best," she managed.

"That's all anyone can ask."

He led the way through the living room and down a long hallway. "The house has five bedrooms. I'm going to give you the two at the back of the house because they have the most privacy. There's a Jack-

and-Jill bathroom between them. This was always sort of the guest suite, so it should suit your needs.''

She had a brief impression of open doors and large bedrooms, then Mitch came to a stop at the end of the hallway. He moved aside to let her enter first.

Alex stepped into a large bedroom with a four-poster bed and a long triple dresser. To the left, a big bay window let in light and had a window seat. The quilt and matching rugs looked handmade and very old. She walked to the bed and touched the pale-pink-and-green quilted squares. The tiny stitches told their own story and she wondered about the women who had spent hours making this gift of the heart.

''It's lovely,'' she said, meaning both the room and the handmade spread.

''It's no palace, but it's clean and quiet. That armoire has a television in it. We have a satellite dish so you can keep up with what's going on back home.''

Alex checked out the walk-in closet. Her clothes would fit nicely. ''I won't have any trouble with that. I'll be sent daily bulletins. Some things will come by fax or e-mail, but the sensitive documents will be hand delivered by a messenger.''

''What's so important that it can't wait until you get home?''

She looked at him and smiled. ''I'm not just a princess. I have official state duties that continue to be my responsibility even when I'm out of the country.''

She crossed to the door leading to the bathroom and stared at the vanity and double sink. Another door led to the toilet and tub. Beyond that was a matching vanity and the study beyond. "So that's what you meant when you said 'Jack-and-Jill' bathroom. I'd never heard the expression before." Mitch had followed her on her inspection tour. She gave a light laugh. "I was half expecting something labeled His and Hers."

"No. Families do this when they have a bunch of kids. It makes it easier for them to share a bathroom without arguing over who's spending too much time at the mirror."

"I see." Although she couldn't. Alex didn't think she'd ever shared a bathroom with anyone.

The sister bedroom to hers had been converted into a study complete with a desk across from a sofa and chair. The matching bay window faced a fenced paddock that held three mares. Alex crossed the room to gaze at them.

The animals grazed in the peaceful afternoon. She felt a flicker of envy. What would it be like to live a life like this one? "It's so quiet here," she said. "When I left Aspen, there were security people everywhere. My sisters were arguing over who got what bedroom, and the cook was complaining because the proper supplies had yet to be delivered. To make it all the more interesting, half the town had already figured out we were in residence, so there was a constant stream of cars driving by the front gates. It's just a matter of time until the press starts camping out."

"If your sisters are as pretty as you, then I can sure understand why. Any of you married?"

It was the second time he'd complimented her.

Over the years she'd been told many positive things about her appearance. Some had been outrageous flattery, and some she'd believed. Even so, no practiced collection of words had made her feel as flustered as this man's casual comments.

"Um, no. We're all still single. I'm the oldest." She smiled. "I've had several rock stars propose, but I've managed to steer clear of any romantic engagements."

He leaned against the door frame, and it seemed as if he held up the wall instead of the other way around. "I can't imagine living like that," he said. "I promise no press or rock stars out here. The most excitement will be when Betty, my housekeeper, finds out you're really a princess. She has a thing for royalty. She follows the British royal family and that one in Monaco."

His gaze drifted over her body again. As he looked at her, she had the oddest sensation of heat and pressure, almost as if he was really touching her skin. How ridiculous, she told herself. It must be jet lag.

"She's going to want to fatten you up," he said.

It took her a minute to figure out who the "she" was. "Your housekeeper?"

"Yeah. Betty's not one for skinny women."

She wanted to ask about his preference, but didn't have the courage. Besides, something wonderfully alive and hot flickered in his eyes. Something that made her mouth go dry and her legs tingle.

Their conversation was far too personal to be appropriate, she thought, trying to distract herself. Yet if she was honest with herself, she would admit that she didn't want to change the subject. Nor did she want to complain about the way Mitch was looking at her. Because very few men bothered to see her as a woman instead of a princess. Alex would have bet her favorite pair of diamond earrings that at that moment he'd completely forgotten she was anything close to royalty.

She had to clear her throat before she could speak. "You have a very lovely home, Mitch, and I'm honored to stay here. Thank you."

"Your watchdog hasn't cleared me yet."

"Is there any doubt?"

He sighed. "Not a one. And I'm a dozen kinds of crazy for letting you move in, princess."

"Will it be so awful?"

His gaze settled on her face. She found herself studying his mouth and wishing it weren't quite so intriguing.

"Awful?" he asked. "No. It's going to be worse."

At exactly seven that evening, as it did every Sunday night, the phone rang. Mitch picked it up on the first ring. "Hi, Mom, hi, Dad," he said into the receiver.

"Mitch!"

His parents greeted him as they always did, their familiar voices bright with pleasure.

"How are things up there?" Mitch asked as he leaned back in his favorite chair and closed his eyes.

He could picture his parents in their quarters in their bed-and-breakfast in the San Juan Islands in Washington state. They'd retired there about five years before with the intent of buying a small house and finally taking things easy. After six months they'd both been going crazy with boredom. As his mother put it, a body couldn't spend a lifetime working from sunup until midnight and then just stop. So they'd purchased a small bed-and-breakfast, fixed it up and started catering to an upscale crowd. They both loved it.

"We're doing well. I have to tell you, though, some days I think cattle are a darn sight easier to deal with than people," his father said.

His mother laughed. "He's just annoyed because some of the guests wouldn't go on his evening walk. You know how your father likes to collect everyone together, then herd them along the path by the cliffs."

"The exercise makes them appreciate their dinners more. It's healthy."

"They're on vacation, Bob. Let them rest."

It was a familiar argument. Enough of one that Mitch allowed himself to be distracted by faint noises coming from the back of the house. He hadn't seen much of his guest since her security team had reluctantly cleared both him and his employees. They'd driven off only a short time ago, and that was after leaving him with pages of written instructions, phone numbers to call in case of emergency and a cell phone that connected automatically with the FBI.

He knew he was going to regret letting Princess Alexandra of Wynborough stay with him, and not just because she was going to be a pain in the butt. He was going to regret it because she was the first woman in a long time who tempted him. He couldn't help staring at her body and wondering what it would feel like next to and under his. He wanted to kiss her and hold her and lick her and—

"Mitch, are you listening?"

His mother's voice broke through his erotic daydream.

"I'm here, Mom."

"Is everything all right?"

He'd decided not to mention his guest to his parents. His mom would get way too excited about royalty, and his dad would figure it was a cover for a hot romance and start talking about grandkids. "Everything's fine. Have you heard from John?"

There was a brief pause. He knew both his folks would be momentarily sad at the thought of their youngest son. They never understood his need to roam, although they respected it and always welcomed him home. "Not in a few weeks."

"Me, either. I've just been thinking about him. If he calls you, will you ask him to phone me?"

"Of course, dear."

They chatted for a few more minutes, then Mitch heard the beep of his call-waiting. "I have another call."

"Go ahead and take it," his father said. "We were about to say goodbye. We love you, son."

"I love you, too. Bye." He pushed the Flash button and connected the waiting call. "Hello?"

"Mitch Colton?" an unfamiliar male voice asked.

"Yes."

"This is Andrew Morgan from the State Department. I'm calling to thank you for extending your hospitality to Princess Alexandra. Our nation ·has a long and cordial history with her country. After the unfortunate loss of their son, the king and queen choose not to visit us. We were deeply disturbed by this. Fortunately, the visit of the princesses allows us an opportunity to make some kind of amends for what happened before. Your nation is very grateful for your cooperation in this matter."

Mitch held the phone in front of him for a second and stared at it disbelievingly before returning it to his ear. This wasn't really happening to him, was it?

"Mr. Colton?"

"Yeah, I'm here. I'm happy to help."

"Good. I have a special phone number for you. Please call with any problems or special requests." The man went on to talk about the importance of making the princess's stay a pleasant one, that FBI security would be instantly available in the event of something going wrong and would Mitch like some information from the Protocol department on how to interact with royalty.

"I think we're doing fine on that one," he said dryly.

"As you wish," Mr. Morgan said. "If you change your mind, you can reach me at the number I gave you. When all this is finished, the government would like to show its gratitude in the form of an invitation to the White House. Perhaps your parents would like to attend with you."

Mitch. would have preferred a cut in his property taxes for the year, but he doubted Andrew wanted to hear that. "Thanks. I'm sure that will be very nice."

"Call me if you have any questions. And again, Mr. Colton, thank you from a grateful nation."

There was a click and then silence. Mitch hung up and swore. Yup, just like he'd thought. Nothing was ever going to be the same again.

Chapter Three

"Are you all right?"

Mitch glanced up and saw that Alex had walked into the living room. She still wore the toast-colored knit dress that clung to her curves in a way that was decidedly unroyal—at least in his masculine opinion. Not that he was going to complain. If he had to have a princess in his house, at least he'd gotten a beautiful one.

"The State Department just phoned," he said. "They wanted to make sure I planned to extend every courtesy to the representative of an important country, or something like that."

She didn't even have the decency to look surprised. Instead she nodded seriously. "I forgot to mention that they would be in touch. It's more of a formality than anything. I wouldn't worry about it."

"I hadn't planned to." He stared at her, taking in the blue eyes and the cascade of auburn curls. Deep inside, the flame of need roared into a full-fledged wildfire. Just his luck. The first woman to get his attention in several years turned out to be about as unapproachable as a nun. "You really are a princess," he grumbled. "So what am I supposed to do with you?"

She gave a soft laugh that threatened his composure. "You could invite me to sit down."

Only then did he realize she was standing. "Sorry." He waved at the sofa, then leaned forward in his chair. "Look, Alex, if you're going to be staying here, you're going to have to just go ahead and do what you want. If you're planning on waiting for me to ask you if you want a drink or something to eat, you're going to starve. I spend most of my days out with the cattle and my evenings working on the books. I don't have much company, certainly not your kind."

"I appreciate the warning. I promise to take care of food and water for myself."

"Except for Sunday, you won't have to worry about food. Betty will be here in the morning and she's going to be thrilled to have someone else to cook for."

"Are you sure I won't be in the way? I don't want to be a bother."

"You won't be," he told her, answering the question in the context she'd intended. After all, she bothered him plenty, but that was his problem and he would solve it all on his own. Her stay was very temporary. When she was gone, he was going to have to force himself to start dating again. Obviously he'd been spending way too much time alone.

"I spoke to my parents," he said. "I didn't tell them about you being here, but I did ask them to have John call me if he got in touch with them."

"That's wonderful. Thank you." She tilted her head. "Why didn't you say anything about me?"

"For one thing, I hadn't talked to you about it. I figured you'd want to keep your presence here as quiet as possible. For another, they wouldn't understand."

She wrinkled her nose slightly. "Because I'm a princess?"

"Because you're a woman."

She raised her eyebrows but otherwise didn't respond to his statement. The lamplight caught on the curls on the top of her head and gave them a goldish glow. Again he saw that she had the most perfect skin and long, slender hands. She moved those hands now to open a folder that he hadn't noticed until just that moment. Inside were more than a dozen sheets of paper.

"There are a couple of items I would like to discuss," she said. "As I mentioned earlier, my parents don't know the real reason my sisters and I are in this country. They think we're here doing publicity for my father's celebration." She looked up and gave him a quick smile. "We are doing that, as well, but our real purpose is to find out information about our brother."

"You're not going to get much publicity out here," he said. Then an ugly thought occurred to him.

"You're not planning on inviting the press to the ranch, are you? I don't want things disrupted more than they have to be."

"Of course not, Mitch. No press, not even an interview. We arranged the schedule so each of us would have some free time to work on the investigation. I have to attend a charity fund-raiser in Los Angeles in a few weeks, but other than that my calendar is clear until after the first of the year."

"You've thought it all out."

"I hope so. This is important to us."

She continued to talk about her plans, but Mitch found himself distracted by the thought of what she was doing. While he believed the story about her brother, in his mind the odds that the kid had survived seemed slim. Did she really think that John might be the long-lost heir to a kingdom? Mitch shook his head. Not John. No way. He was a drifter, someone who had, despite the family's best efforts, never fit in. If he was Alex's brother, wouldn't he behave royally or something?

"I've already made arrangements for the extra phone lines," Alex was saying.

"You got through to the phone company on a Sunday?" he asked.

"I didn't call the phone company directly. I was given a special number. They're going to have to run another trunk line to the house." She paused. "I'm not sure what that means, but I'm hoping it won't be too disruptive. Of course, I'll cover any costs involved."

He waved her comment away. "Don't worry about it."

"All right. The rest of my things will be here on Tuesday. The office equipment, the computer, copy machine and fax will arrive tomorrow. Then there's the messenger service. They'll be delivering daily, sometimes twice a day."

Mitch leaned back in his chair and tried not to let his dismay show. Just as he'd thought, his life was being pulled in a direction he didn't want to go. "You're not going to start playing polo on the front lawn, are you?"

Alex glanced up. "I don't play polo."

Her accent intrigued him. He wanted to hear her say his name softly, but with passion. Down boy, he told himself. Don't go there.

"If you don't mind, I'd like to ask you some questions about your brother," she said, flipping to another page in her folder. "You both went to school locally." She read for a second. "You played sports quite a bit, I see, as did John. Football? That's different from soccer or English rugby. I've actually seen a few games live. It's a little confusing, but I liked it."

He stared at her, then at the papers in her hands. He'd assumed she just had lists of whatever princesses kept lists of, but it wasn't that at all. Irritation built inside him until it pushed him to his feet and across the room.

"May I?" he asked, even as he took the folder from her. He scanned the contents of several sheets. There were detailed histories of himself and his family members, information on the ranch employees and even copies of his last three tax returns.

"What the hell is all this?" he asked, tossing it back at her.

Alex grabbed the papers and stared up at Mitch with some surprise. His change from cordial host to hostile adversary startled her. "Is there some mistake? Did they get something wrong?"

He planted his hands on his hips and glared down at her. She suddenly felt small and faintly alarmed.

"No. They got everything right."

"Then I don't understand the problem."

"That *is* the problem."

She studied him for a couple of seconds, then realization dawned. "Oh, I see. You're upset because I have this information. What's the expression? You consider it an invasion of your privacy?"

"Damn straight."

She drew in a deep breath. It was easy to forget that the rest of the world was different from her reality. "If you would stop looming over me, I could try to explain."

Despite his obvious irritation, he flashed her a quick grin. "I'm looming?"

"Rather impressively. I'm tall, and most men are my height or shorter. You're taller by several inches. I'm not used to that."

He sank onto the far end of the sofa. "We grow them big out West."

"So I've heard." She closed the folder and smoothed the cover. "I'm sorry this has upset you. I never thought it would be a problem, but that's because I have very little privacy of my own. I often forget the rest of the world isn't like that.''

"I guess I can understand that,'' he said.

Alex searched his face. She sensed that he was saying the right words, but that he didn't really mean them. She wanted him to understand. She not only needed his cooperation to help her find her brother, but she and Mitch were going to be living in the same house for a short period of time. It would be easier if they could get along.

"I know this isn't anything you expected or wanted. One minute you were living your life and the next I invaded it. I do hope we can find a way to make this work for both of us.''

His gaze sharpened suddenly, as if her words had a meaning that only he could understand. Then he rose to his feet. "You're right. I didn't ask for you to be here, but you're here now so there's no point in complaining. As for making this work, I suggest we try to stay out of each other's way as much as possible. The ranch is big enough, as is the house.'' He headed for the door.

"Mitch, wait.'' She gestured to the folder. "I still have more questions. I'm not finished with you.''

He paused and looked her up and down. "Maybe not, princess, but I'm finished with you.''

Alex compared the numbers on the computer screen in front of her to the papers that had arrived earlier that morning by messenger. Donations to the Wynborough children's organization she ran were up considerably. The new advertising campaign was a success. She made a note to send the publicity director a handwritten thank-you letter, then went to the next item on her list.

She'd been on the ranch four days and finally had things organized. Setting up a remote office had taken longer than she'd expected, but now she was able to stay in touch with the palace and her sisters. Now if only the mysterious John Colton would make an appearance.

She heard the sound of approaching footsteps in the hallway and glanced at the clock on her desk. It was nearly ten, so the visitor would be Betty with her morning coffee.

"You don't have to do this," Alex said as she rose to greet the other woman. "I've told you, I'm not a real guest here. I'm more of an intrusion."

Betty, an attractive woman in her mid-fifties, waved her off with a smile. "I haven't had anyone to spoil in ages. Mitch is always working, and there's never anyone else around to cook for. I like it. Besides, when all this is over, I get to tell all my friends about taking care of a real live princess."

As she had for the past couple of days, Betty set the tray with two cups of coffee and some incredibly delicious cookies that she made herself. The two women moved to the sofa at the far end of the study and sat down. Alex enjoyed both the break from her work and the company. Despite Betty's short gray hair, the woman had a youthful glint in her eyes and a wicked sense of humor. She also knew everything about the ranch.

"Are you all settled?" Betty asked.

Alex took a sip of coffee and nodded. "I was able to get right to work this morning. I'm trying to clear up as much of my work as possible so I can get on with the investigation. What with coming over to America, then moving to the ranch, I'm a little behind." She glanced at the piles of papers on her desk. "I'm in touch with the palace several times a day. There's so much to organize."

"Almost sounds like you're running a company."

"In a way it's very similar." Alex pressed her lips together. "I spoke to my parents this morning. I haven't done that since moving here."

Betty nodded sympathetically. "Did they accept your story about taking some time to relax at a private ranch resort?"

Alex nodded. She'd had to come up with a way to explain a different area code and phone number to her parents. Betty had been the one to suggest saying she'd gone away to unwind for a couple of weeks. "It was horrible. They were both pleased I was taking time for myself."

"What's wrong with that? They sound like lovely people."

"Oh, they are, but I'm not used to lying to them. It's not something I do often or well. I just felt uncomfortable." She took another sip of coffee, then sampled one of the chocolate chip cookies on the tray. "But I reminded myself it was for a greater good. If we find James, they'll understand. If we don't, better that they aren't troubled by what we're doing."

Betty leaned forward. "I think it's very exciting

that you're searching for your long-lost brother. I hope it turns out to be John.''

''That would be convenient,'' Alex admitted. ''But there's only a one-in-three chance of it being him. I want to get over to The Sunshine Home and go through their records. I finally have permission from the current owner. Although, she warned me that nothing that old has been put on computer, so it's going to have to be a manual search. We're going to have to find the other two boys who arrived around the same time as John.''

Alex paused and took another bite of the sweet cookie. ''There's so much to coordinate. And as if searching for my long-lost brother isn't enough, I worry about my sisters, especially Serena.''

''She's the youngest?'' Betty asked.

''Yes. She has a wild streak that is going to get her into trouble. And there's something wrong with Elizabeth, although I can't figure out what.'' Alex thought about the conversation she'd had with Elizabeth just that morning. Her sister had seemed distracted again. ''Right now the only one I can count on is Katherine.''

''I've seen their pictures in the paper. They're all very pretty young women. I'm surprised you all aren't married.''

''Sometimes we are, too,'' Alex admitted. She glanced around the homey room. The decorations had a woman's touch. ''Did you and Mitch's mother decorate the house?''

''Most of it. Now that she's moved away, I don't change things as much as I used to. Mitch's study is off-limits, of course, as is his bedroom. That man is incredibly stubborn about certain things.''

He might be stubborn, Alex thought, but he was also a man of his word. He'd told her that they should stay out of each other's way, and so far that was exactly what he'd done. She'd barely seen him since Sunday, and when she had sought him out to ask him a question, he grunted rather than answered. Telling herself it was silly didn't make the faint sensation of disappointment go away. Foolishly she'd thought they could be friends.

She glanced at Betty. The housekeeper had known Mitch since he was a boy. Alex had thought about asking her about him, but hadn't quite worked up the nerve or the right question. Impulsively she decided she might as well plunge in with both feet.

''I'm surprised Mitch isn't married.''

Betty snorted. ''I keep telling him he needs a woman around here, but he doesn't listen. Of course, there aren't that many to choose from in the area, and city girls don't usually take to ranch life.'' Her gaze turned speculative. ''You're different enough from...'' She shook her head. ''Never mind. I won't discuss his personal business.''

Alex brushed her hand self-consciously against her wool skirt, then touched the cuff of her silk blouse. *What* personal business? she wanted to ask, but didn't.

''No. It wouldn't work at all.'' Betty set her cup on the tray and started to laugh. ''I had a moment of being crazy. Oil and water. A fancy woman and a simple man.'' Betty chuckled again. ''I mean simple in his ways, not in his head. Mitch is about as smart as they come.''

Alex realized that Betty had wondered about her and Mitch. ''You're right, it wouldn't work. You should have seen the look he gave me when I asked him about covered parking for my car.''

''You've changed things for him, and he doesn't much like that. But give him time. Sometimes the grumpy old bear can be sweet as pie.''

''I'd settle for an actual conversation,'' Alex said.

Betty smiled and rose to her feet. ''I have some fresh salmon. Would you like that for lunch?''

''How nice. Thank you.''

''I'll see you in a few hours,'' Betty said, then left.

Alex stood up, but instead of returning to her desk, she crossed to the window. From there she could see out to the paddocks by the barn. Mitch stood there, talking with two other men. She couldn't hear what he was saying, but she could see the gestures he made as he spoke. The other two listened with obvious respect.

She told herself it didn't matter what he thought of her. She was here because she had to find out the truth about her brother. But even though she believed the words, she didn't like them. She didn't want Mitch to resent her presence on his ranch. Unfortunately, she didn't know how to change things. She was great at large-party small talk and giving speeches about needy children, but one-on-one with a man was a mystery.

To make matters worse, she didn't even think Mitch liked her. At first she'd thought he had, but something had changed and she didn't know what. If she didn't know what was wrong, she couldn't know how to fix it.

"It doesn't matter," she told herself, speaking aloud. "I have work to do."

So she returned to her desk, but it was a long time before she could forget the handsome cowboy outside and focus on the details of the report in front of her.

Chapter Four

Mitch held out his coffee mug but didn't say anything as Betty filled the cup. The bad mood that hovered over him like a cloud had him seeing no point in inflicting himself on his housekeeper. This despite the fact that she was going out of her way to bait him.

"You know she has the most beautiful jewelry," Betty was saying. "She showed me several pieces. There are some diamonds and pearls and even this tiara that's been in her family for nearly four hundred years. Can you imagine?"

"Not really," Mitch grumbled. "Can we talk about something else?"

"Like what?" Betty's expression was all innocence, but he knew her better than that. She'd figured out that talking about Alex bugged him, so she was doing it as much as she dared.

"I don't get the fascination," he said, glaring at her. "The woman is a menace. She's taken over the ranch like she's the new owner."

"That's hardly true," Betty protested. "She barely leaves her office."

"Why should she? Everyone comes to her. If it's not a messenger service arriving two and three times a day, it's the phone ringing at all hours. I feel like I'm living in a hotel. A man can barely get a decent meal these days."

Betty raised her eyebrows as she placed his steaming breakfast in front of him. It was just past six in the morning, but she'd already prepared him eggs, bacon and pancakes. "Are you complaining about my cooking?"

"No." He wasn't going to get Betty annoyed with him. He'd done that a couple of times before and had suffered through a series of vegetarian casseroles and tofu stir-fries until he'd had the good sense to apologize.

"I didn't think so." She poured herself coffee and settled in the seat opposite his. "I don't see what the problem is. Princess Alexandra is a wonderful young woman. I'm proud to know her."

"Good for you."

Nothing was going the way it was supposed to, he thought glumly. He'd hoped that by avoiding the woman in question, he would forget about his attraction to her. Unfortunately, not physically being in the same room wasn't enough. He caught glimpses of her from time to time. On a working ranch where everyone wore jeans and sensible boots, including Betty,

Alex dressed in silk shirts and long, swaying skirts. When he couldn't see her, he could hear her voice. When he couldn't hear her, he could smell her. That damn perfume of hers permeated the house like a stink bomb. The sweet scent was everywhere. If he didn't know better, he would swear that Betty was washing his sheets in the damn stuff.

He was spending so much time trying *not* to think about her that she ended up being the only thing he *did* think about. He was thirty-three years old, and he had it worse than he'd ever had it at seventeen.

"I think Princess Alexandra is doing her best to fit in," Betty said. "After all, this is her first trip to our country. We should try to make her feel at home."

"No one has to try to do anything. She's at home, all right. She's the one running the show around here."

"If you have a complaint, you should take it up with Princess Alexandra directly."

He slammed his mug onto the table and ignored the coffee that sloshed over onto his hand. "Would you stop calling her that!"

"What?" Betty was innocence personified. In a pig's eye, he thought.

"Princess Alexandra. She wants to be called Alex."

"I like her title. She doesn't mind that I use it, so you shouldn't, either."

"You're only doing it to bug me."

Betty smiled. "Maybe, but only because you've earned it. If you have any beefs, why don't you take them up directly with her?"

He picked up a fork and stabbed his steaming eggs. "Alex is imperious, snotty, bossy and always expects to get her way. Look at what she has you cooking for her. What was that thing you made for lunch yesterday?"

Betty stole a strip of bacon from his plate and munched on it. "Salmon with penne pasta in a cream sauce, steamed baby vegetables and crème brûlée for dessert. Speaking of dessert, I saw you ate two, so don't try to tell me you didn't like it."

"I did like it, but that's not the point. You're not her personal chef. You shouldn't have to spend so much time catering to her."

"I enjoy the challenge," Betty said. "If you had your way, you'd eat steak and baked potatoes every night. How exciting is that?"

"It's plain, simple food. Good enough for me and my family. What about the wine? It's all imported. How much is it costing me?"

"She brought her own wine with her. As for it being imported, most of it is from California, or so you'd know if you bothered to look instead of casting blame where it doesn't belong. If you want my opinions, I think she irritates you so much because you're two peas in a pod."

He nearly choked on his mouthful of pancakes. When he'd finished chewing, he swallowed and glared at her. "What?"

"You heard me. You think the princess is imperious and wants to get her own way? Well, the only reason you recognize those particular qualities is that you have them yourself. Looking in the emotional mirror is always painful.''

''I am not imperious,'' he said loudly. ''I'm a nice guy. Everyone likes me. I do not tell other people what to do.''

Betty's only response was to raise her eyebrows.

''I'm very easygoing,'' Mitch insisted.

''This from a man who got upset because I served him ham on Wednesday instead of Thursday?'' Her voice was sweetly smug.

''That happened once. It was years ago.''

''It was last month, and if you want other examples I have dozens.''

He opened his mouth to respond, but just then he heard footsteps in the hallway. The princess was up and ready for her breakfast.

''Some of us have to work for a living,'' he said, and tossed his napkin on top of his half-eaten breakfast. He pushed back from the table, then grabbed his hat as he headed for the door.

Betty started laughing. ''I never thought I'd see the day when you were chased out of your own house by a woman, Mitch.''

''I'm not being chased, I'm leaving.''

''One day you'll have to explain the difference,'' she said with a chuckle.

Alex heard both laughter and the slamming of the back door as she entered the kitchen. She glanced out the window in time to see Mitch heading for the garage next to the barn. No doubt he would get in his four-wheel-drive truck and be gone for the entire day.

For reasons she didn't quite understand, she had to fight back a sigh of sadness. Foolishly she'd hoped they might have breakfast together this morning. She'd gotten up a little earlier than usual in hopes of catching him. If she didn't know better, she would say that Mitch Colton was avoiding her.

"Care to share the joke?" she asked as she walked over to the counter by the stove and poured herself a cup of coffee.

Betty grinned at her. "That man is the most stubborn person on the planet. He's all in a temper about you, which is really due to the fact that he's suddenly not the center of the universe. He's complaining that you're bossy and always expecting to get your way." Betty winked. "Of course, what he refuses to see is that the person he's describing is himself."

Years of training allowed Alex to maintain a neutral expression, but inside she felt shock. Betty's easy chatter and good humor meant that the housekeeper didn't think she was saying anything extraordinary, so she wasn't trying to be insulting.

"Bossy?" Alex asked, forcing herself to smile slightly.

Betty rose from the table and crossed to stand next to Alex. "Actually I said imperious. I think that fits better."

Alex wasn't sure if they were talking about Mitch or herself and she didn't dare ask. "I'm sorry I'm annoying him."

Betty waved off her apology. "Don't give it a thought. All this activity is good for him. Mitch has spent too much time on his own these past couple of years. He's needed something or someone to shake him out of his rut. If it takes a fancy-pants princess to do it, then I say, well done.''

A fancy-pants princess, Alex thought incredulously. Is that how Betty perceived her? It was all she could do not to walk back to her bedroom and start packing. Had she expected too much of her host and his housekeeper? She knew there had been some unusual requests, but she'd tried to keep them to a minimum. The problem was she had no point of reference. She'd never lived a regular life, so she didn't know what was normal and what wasn't.

''Have I been too demanding?'' Alex asked. ''If the cooking is too much trouble or—''

Betty cut her off with a quick shake of her head. ''Don't go thinking that,'' she said firmly. ''I've had a wonderful time talking with you every day, and I've enjoyed stretching my cooking skills. I get to try different recipes and ingredients. Mitch isn't one to eat fancy food so I get bored fixing the same few things.'' She grinned. ''Of course, he's going to squeal like a stuck pig when he gets the food bill, but that will be fun, too.''

Alex leaned against the counter as the next wave of shock raced through her. She thought about all the wonderful dishes Betty had prepared. The housekeeper always discussed the menus with Alex and offered suggestions. Because it was so close to how things were done in the castle, Alex hadn't given it another thought. But this was Arizona, not Wynborough, and an isolated ranch wasn't going to have easy access to continental cuisine.

"Of course I'll reimburse Mr. Colton for the additional expense," she said stiffly as she thought of messengers who made their trips out here several times a day, of the fax and the computer set up in the second guest room, of the phone calls and the additional phone lines she'd had installed.

"Don't worry about that," Betty told her. "Mitch can afford it. Besides, he's eating the same food you are, and I haven't heard a single complaint out of him. He's just bellyaching. It doesn't mean anything."

"Thanks for telling me that," Alex said. She made a show of checking her watch. "I'm expecting a fax, so I'll just take my coffee back to the office." She turned to leave.

"Don't you want breakfast?" Betty asked.

"Not this morning. Thank you."

Alex knew she would choke if she tried to force anything down her throat. She could feel the flush of embarrassment on her face as humiliation filled her. Perhaps it would have meant her parents finding out what was going on, but she should have gone to a hotel. Staying here at the Colton ranch had been a horrible mistake. She saw that now. Why hadn't she realized what an imposition she would be?

She made it back to her desk before the trembling began. Now what? she asked herself. Should she leave? Rowan would be furious at her and he would hate having to find another secure location, but she didn't see any other choice. She couldn't stay here and continue to be a bother to Mitch. No wonder he'd been avoiding her.

She reached for a pad of paper to start a list, but

the phone rang. As she picked up the receiver, she wondered how she could have been so incredibly insensitive.

"I thought I'd save you the trouble of having to phone in yourself later," a familiar voice said.

"Mother," she breathed in relief. "How are you?"

"Fine, as usual. In the midst of chaos, also as usual." Her mother's light laughter trilled across the thousands of miles. "It's still raining, so the renovations are slowing and that's making everyone irritable. Especially your father. You know how he gets."

Alex did know. She listened as her mother talked about what was going on at home, then took notes on a few governmental issues that concerned her. Finally, when they were about to say goodbye, Alex hesitated. "I have a question," she said.

"What is it, dear?"

"Am I..." Her voice trailed off as she thought back to what Betty had said. "Am I bossy and imperious?"

Her mother laughed again. "Of course you are, but we love you anyway."

Alex was glad she was sitting down. She felt her mouth drop open. "You're being serious? I've always thought of myself as responsible. Was I wrong?"

"No, Alexandra. You're very responsible. You're a warm and caring person. Your father and I are very proud of you. You take your duties seriously, and we can always depend on you to do the right thing. Occasionally your methods are a little high-handed, but you're the oldest daughter of a king. Isn't that to be expected?"

Her mother spoke for a few more minutes, then said her goodbyes. Alex replaced the receiver, then leaned back in her chair. Did everyone think the same about her? That she was dutiful and responsible, but in a high-handed way? Did everyone hate her? Had she been deceiving herself about her personality?

The unexpected information caused her to think about dozens of incidents from her past. She replayed them in light of the new information and still wasn't sure what to think. Finally, close to noon, she went for a walk.

While it might be raining in Wynborough, it was a beautiful, clear day in Arizona. The air was chilly, but dry. There weren't any clouds and the nearby mountains stood like silent sentinels. She inhaled the scent of cattle and horses, of trees and brush, of the fresh air preparing for winter and the distant promise of snow.

She'd pulled a wool jacket over her blouse, and she tucked her hands into the front pockets. Her boots crunched on the scattered leaves that littered the path to the main barn. The door stood open, so she walked inside. To the left were the tack room and feed bins, to the right, the horse stalls. She turned right and walked down the center aisle. Curious horses popped their heads over half doors to watch their visitor.

Alex paused to pet a beautiful bay mare. She stroked the animal's smooth face and soft nose. Big brown eyes stared at her.

"Hi, pretty lady," she murmured. "You have a very lovely ranch here. Did you know that? I didn't. Until just now I'd barely left the house."

The horse stomped in response. Alex felt some of her tension easing, although not her pain and confusion. About an hour before, Laura had called her from Aspen with an update on her sisters. Alex had forced herself to ask her social secretary the same question she'd asked her mother. The several heartbeats of silence followed by Laura's insincere, "No, of course not," had told their own story. Didn't anyone like her?

"What's wrong?"

Alex jumped at the sound of the male voice. She turned suddenly and saw Mitch standing in the center of the aisle. "I didn't hear you come in," she said.

"So I guessed." His dark gaze regarded her steadily. "I was driving back from the range when I saw you walk in here. You don't make it a habit to visit the horses, so I thought I'd come see what was going on."

"I won't hurt them," she said quickly, feeling defensive. "I just wanted to get out of the office for a little bit. I've always ridden, English not Western, but I'm good around horses."

"I'm not saying you're not," Mitch said, holding up his hands in a gesture of surrender. "I meant I thought there was something wrong. With you, not with them."

He took a step closer. She could see the powerful muscles in his thighs bunching and releasing with the movement. He was so tall and so strong. He was also a stranger who resented her presence in his home.

"I..." She pressed her lips together and tried to figure out what she was supposed to say. She opened her mouth again, but this time the words that tumbled out were not what she expected. "Everyone thinks I'm bossy and imperious and I'm afraid they might be right."

"This is news to you?"

"Well, yes." To her horror, she felt her eyes begin to burn. She blinked to hold back the tears. She never cried. "I'm a good person. I work hard. I take my responsibilities seriously. I have a sense of humor. People like me."

"So it's a trade-off."

She glared at him. "I see you're very happy to discuss my problems, but what about the fact that you're exactly the same? Except, possibly, for having a sense of humor. I haven't seen any evidence of that."

"Hey, wait a minute." Mitch took another step closer and glared down at her. "I'm not bossy, I'm the world's nicest guy. Just ask anyone. Just because you don't like what you see in the mirror is no reason to blame me."

"I like what I see in the mirror just fine."

"Then why are you upset?"

"I'm not upset." She planted her hands on her hips. "You're the one who won't even consider the truth about himself. Is self-inspection so frightening? Is the macho facade all you have going for you?"

"Macho facade?" Mitch repeated. "Listen, princess, it's not a facade. As for my sense of humor, it's a hell of a lot more developed than yours."

"How would you know?"

"Because you're just some—" He broke off and stared at her.

"Some what?"

His stiff body posture relaxed a little. "I don't know. I want to compare you to something, but I don't know you well enough to do that. Maybe you could give me a hint so I could come up with an insult and we could continue arguing."

His outrageous request made her smile. Then he grinned and before she could figure out how it had happened, all her tension eased. Her arms relaxed and she found herself breathing easily for the first time in hours.

Mitch joined her at the mare's stall. "You've got some backbone...for a princess," he said condescendingly.

"Thank you. You're not so very annoying...for a man."

He growled low in his throat. "I'm going to ignore that."

"It's probably for the best. Otherwise you'd be forced to think about it and that might tax your brain."

"You're on a tear this morning, aren't you?"

"I suppose I am." She shoved her hands back into her jacket pocket. "I'm moving to a hotel."

He stared at her. "Why?"

"It's for the best. I didn't realize what an intrusion I would be. It was the tiniest bit imperious of me to insist on staying here. You don't know me, we aren't related. You didn't ask for any of this." She thought about all the arrangements that had to be made. "It will probably take a couple of days to get everything put together, but I'll be gone as quickly as I can."

"What about your parents? I thought you didn't want to have to explain extra security."

"I'll think of something. I always do." She glanced around at the clean, well-lit barn and wished she'd taken the time to explore the area. "I appreciate your hospitality. You've been very kind."

Mitch mumbled something she didn't quite catch. He turned his attention back to the mare. "You've got everything in place, the phone lines, the messengers. If it's not going to get any worse, you might as well stay."

As gracious invitations went, she'd had much better. Even so, his words lightened her spirits and made her insides tingle in the most unusual way. "But—"

He glared at her. "Don't make me beg, okay? Because I won't do it. You can stay here."

He was a grumpy old bear, she thought. But handsome. His mouth still intrigued her, as did his strength. "Thank you," she murmured.

"You're welcome."

His gaze lingered on her face. It warmed her like a touch...or a caress. The tingling inside of her spread to her arms and legs. She told herself to stop staring, but she couldn't seem to look away from him. The rest of the world faded into a blurry background. How odd.

"Mitch?"

He took a step toward her. She had to look up to still meet his gaze, but instead of intimidating her, his size made her feel safe. She noticed her breathing had quickened, as had his. What was wrong with them?

Mitch swore under his breath. ''I've got to get back to work,'' he growled.

''Can I help?'' Alex asked, surprising both him and herself. She glanced around the barn. ''As I said, I'm good with horses. Maybe I could exercise them for you.'' She bit her lower lip. ''I can't seem to fill my days enough with the work I have,'' she admitted. That was as much as she could say. She refused to tell him that she was lonely.

He pointed to her tailored wool skirt. ''Are all your clothes that impractical?''

''No. I have a brand-new pair of jeans with me.''

''Figures. All right, you can exercise a couple of the mares, but only on a lead. No fancy riding until I see what you can do.''

She smiled at him. ''Thank you, Mitch. You won't regret it.''

She turned and headed for the house, ignoring his grumbled complaint that he already did.

Five hours later Mitch knew he'd been stupid in allowing Alex to exercise the horses. Not that she didn't know what she was doing, he thought as he stared out his office window and looked at the west paddock. She stood in the center of the ring and exercised a brood mare. Despite their difference in size, there was no doubt who was in charge of the session. Alex held the lead with a skill that only came from hours of practice. She hadn't lied about knowing her way around horses.

She also hadn't lied about the jeans, although they were painfully new. He found himself catching his breath as she turned in the ring, exposing her back to him. The stiff denim outlined rounded hips and thighs that just about sent him to his knees. He had a difficult enough time dealing with his wayward desire when he couldn't see her, but now that she was in plain sight he thought he would go mad.

To make matters worse, he was starting to like her. Lust was safe, but liking—well, that was a different story. Liking led to caring which was a slick downhill road to heartache and trouble. Her earlier confession about being bossy had touched him, although he couldn't quite figure out why. Maybe it was her vulnerability, or the strength it took to see a bad truth about one's self.

He should have let her go. She'd offered to leave, but he'd had to tell her to stay because—he didn't even know why he'd done it. So now he was stuck with her and her perfect little fanny. The worst part was, there wasn't one thing he could do about her, except continue to stay out of her way. Anything else was impossible. So that was what he was going to do. Ignore her.

Chapter Five

It was a little after six when Mitch heard Alex walk by his office door. He glanced down at the report he'd been compiling, then at the clock above the fireplace in the far corner. Since Alex had arrived, he'd taken his meals later than usual so that he could avoid seeing her. He told himself it was because he preferred to eat alone rather than make idle small talk with someone he didn't know. The real reason had been because he didn't want to spend any more time than necessary in her presence. The attraction was difficult enough to control without fueling it with actual contact.

But something had changed, he thought as he tossed down his pencil and rose to his feet. That morning when they spoke, he'd seen her more as a person than as a woman he wanted. Dangerous territory, but one he apparently couldn't avoid. Besides, if he was completely honest with himself, he would be willing to admit that he was lonely. John was never around much in the evenings, even when he was home, and Betty left at six. Since his folks had moved up to Washington, there wasn't anyone to talk with once his workday ended. Betty kept ragging on him to get married, but he didn't think he wanted to. Besides, how many woman actually got excited at the thought of living on a relatively isolated ranch?

He crossed the room and headed down the hall. Dating, he thought. He could start dating again. But the idea didn't thrill him. The ranch demanded long hours, which made it difficult for him to meet anyone. He would want to get involved with an intelligent woman, someone challenging, but feminine. It wasn't as if that sort of female simply showed up in a man's life.

He stepped into the dining room. Alex glanced up at him, surprise clear on her face. She'd changed out of her jeans and workshirt. Instead she wore a dark purple dress with long sleeves and a high neck. Glittery combs held her hair back from her face. Dark amethysts glinted from her earlobes. He found he had to clear his throat before he could speak.

"I thought you might like some company for dinner."

She smiled that same damn smile that about drove him to his knees. "That would be delightful," she said.

Delightful, he repeated silently an hour later as they lingered over coffee. Alex was everything he'd feared—charming, witty and easy to talk to. He did *not* need this kind of trouble in his life.

"What did you think?" she asked, motioning to the empty bottle of wine sitting on the table.

"Very nice." He glanced at the label, then at her. "It's from California. I thought royalty had to drink French wine," he teased.

She leaned toward him and lowered her voice. "We do. I'm actually breaking the law every time I take a sip. It's my lone rebellion."

"Do your parents know?"

"I think they suspect, but they don't want to confront me about it and learn the truth. All those years of governesses and finishing schools and I still prefer a good California wine to one produced in France."

"I'm sure they're shocked." He leaned back in his chair. "Did you really go to finishing school?"

"No, I went to a university in England. But we had plenty of instruction on the proper way to behave in all situations. I know the correct placement of glasses and flatware for official functions, the proper gift to send for an assortment of occasions, how to handle potentially damaging social blunders. I can even bake bread."

"I'm impressed."

She tucked a loose strand of hair behind her right ear. "I don't think so, but I do believe you think it's mildly interesting. Our lives are different."

They sat at one end of the long dining room table, Mitch at the head and Alex to his right. When they'd finished eating, Mitch pushed his plate toward the center of the table and Alexandra followed his lead.

Then they leaned forward, facing each other. Now, he watched the play of the overhead light on Alex's face, which made her green eyes appear dark, but added shades of gold to her auburn hair.

"I love this room," she confessed. "When it's quiet, I imagine I can hear conversations from a long time ago. There's been a lot of happiness around this table."

"That's true. My family always ate here for special occasions."

She straightened, and her mouth twisted with dismay. "Oh, no. Please don't tell me that you usually take all your meals in the kitchen."

He nodded.

"I had no idea. Betty brought me out here that first night and I thought…" Her voice trailed off. "Sorry. All that etiquette training doesn't seem to be helping me much out here, does it?"

"I don't mind eating here, Alex. You're right, there are a lot of happy memories. I'm sure the room misses being used. When my folks still lived here, they would have lots of dinner parties. Nothing formal, but plenty of friends and good conversation. I remember Christmas and Thanksgiving dinners here with too much food and extra places for unexpected guests."

She leaned toward him again, resting her elbow on the table and her chin in her hand. "That sounds nice. You're still close with your parents, aren't you?"

"Yes. We speak every week. They call at seven on Sunday evenings. They both get on the phone and tell me about their week. We talk about their guests at their bed-and-breakfast, then we talk about the cattle. It's not very exciting, but it's familiar and I like it.''

''How lovely that sounds,'' she said wistfully. ''When I was a little girl, I used to dream about being in a normal family.''

''Most little girls dream about being a princess.''

''I know. I used to tell myself that whenever I started complaining about something in my life. I was, and am, very fortunate. But sometimes I think how nice it would be to just fit in like everyone else.'' She straightened. ''I'm not saying my parents aren't wonderful people. They are. They're caring and loving and extremely supportive. But it's different.''

''I can't even imagine,'' he said, and meant it. Her world was an alien place, and not one he wanted to visit.

''Mitch, do you have pictures of your family?''

He grinned. ''We have enough photo albums to fill the Library of Congress.''

She frowned. ''The what?''

''Never mind. Yes, there are tons of pictures. Tell you what. You go get dessert and bring it into the living room and I'll grab the photo albums. That is, if I'm allowed to give royalty instructions.''

''Please,'' she said as she rose to her feet. ''Although, if you insist on being impertinent, you run the risk of being beheaded.''

''You still do that sort of thing?''

She gave him a quick grin. ''Daily.''

''Wow. And here I was planning a visit to Wynborough. Guess I'll have to pass.''

''Don't worry. If you do something wrong and are

in danger of being beheaded, just mention my name. I have a little pull with the royal family.''

"Really?''

She made an X over her heart. "I swear.''

Mitch turned a page in album and pointed to a five-by-seven picture. "That's my brother, John.''

Alex stared down at the photograph of the young boy standing next to a horse. She studied the face, the eyes, the shape of the mouth, searching for some similarity. "How old was he here?''

"Probably around ten. What do you think?''

She pressed her lips together. "I'm not sure. I want to say there's something familiar about his expression, but I can't tell if I'm seeing what's there or if it's wishful thinking on my part.''

Mitch patted the album. "There are a dozen more pictures of him. Maybe the ones when he's older will help more.''

"Maybe,'' she agreed, then leaned forward and picked up her mug of coffee.

They'd moved to the living room and were sitting next to each other on the sofa in front of the fireplace. Mitch had started a fire, which now crackled cheerfully. The scent of wood smoke, the lingering taste of chocolate from Betty's decadent mousse, the warmth of the man sitting so close to her all gave Alex an odd feeling of belonging. Which didn't make any sense. After all, she hadn't even been at the ranch for a week. Yet she felt at home here, especially now that she and Mitch were getting along better.

Mitch flipped to the next page. He and John stood

next to each other. Mitch held a first-place ribbon in his hand. "What's that for?" she asked.

"Junior rodeo. Bronc riding and calf roping."

She glanced at him and smiled. "Very impressive."

He shrugged off the compliment. "I grew up on a ranch. It came with the territory."

She turned her attention to the second boy in the picture. Again she couldn't tell if John had any of the family features. "The problem is my sisters and I don't all look alike," she said. "So there's no reason to think our brother would be instantly recognizable. It's a thirty-year-old mystery. Maybe we're fooling ourselves into thinking that we can find out what happened."

"Don't give up," Mitch said. "You've got some new information and you still have The Sunshine Home to investigate. You'll find out what happened."

"I hope so. The owner said the boxes of records would be available next week. They're being delivered from a storage facility. I'm looking forward to going through them."

He continued to turn pages. She watched as Mitch and his brother grew up from gangly boys into handsome young men. There were family Christmases and different birthdays. One picture showed a very serious Mitch in a black tuxedo standing next to a pretty blonde.

"School dance," he said by way of explanation. "I was sixteen."

"Your school put on dances? For the students?"

''Sure. A couple every year. It was a big deal. Did the royal set do that sort of thing?''

He was close enough that his broad shoulder occasionally brushed against hers. She liked the contact and had to consciously keep herself from leaning into him each time. ''No. There were formal occasions such as fund-raisers and balls, but nothing just for the teenagers. That would have been a lot of fun.''

''You sure were raised different.''

That made her laugh. ''It comes with the territory.''

She turned the next page and froze when she saw a wedding photo. Mitch stood next to a pretty young woman in a white bridal gown. There were a half dozen bridesmaids and groomsmen, along with both sets of parents.

''You were married?'' she asked, not sure why she found the information shocking, but she did.

''Yeah, it was a long time ago.'' He took the album from her and closed it. ''It's late. You probably want to head on up to bed.''

She shifted back into the corner of the sofa and angled toward him. ''Don't for a moment think you're going to get rid of me that easily. I had no idea you'd been married before. Betty never said a word.''

Mitch set the album on the coffee table. He drew in a breath as if to speak, but instead was silent. She studied the shaggy brown hair that tumbled down his forehead and the strong line of his nose. While he was a very nice man and a good host, she couldn't figure out why her chest had tightened when she'd learned he'd been married. Nothing about their relationship explained the sharp pain inside or her sudden sense of being betrayed. What was wrong with her? She and Mitch didn't have a personal relationship. His past shouldn't matter to her at all.

Except it did matter, and in ways she couldn't understand.

"It was a long time ago," he said slowly. "Betty teases me, but she's also protective. She wouldn't have talked about it with anyone." He paused. "I was twenty-four when Rose and I married, and although I looked like a man, I was still very much a kid. Most of the reason the marriage failed is I was a jerk. I wanted everything my way, and when that didn't happen I disconnected. I'm not proud of what happened, but I accept responsibility for it. By the time I'd grown up enough to figure out that marriage is a partnership requiring both parties to give back, I'd lost her."

"You're divorced." Alex wasn't asking a question. She was still stunned by what she'd learned, but Mitch's explanation made her feel a little better. She admired his ability to see his part in the failure of the relationship.

"Have been for years now. She's remarried and has a couple of kids."

"Do you miss her?"

Mitch thought about that question. He normally didn't like getting caught up in the past. "Not in the way you mean," he said. "I'm sorry that I was such a jerk and that I lost something that could have been pretty wonderful. But I'm not still in love with her. I'm glad Rose was able to find someone to appreciate her."

Alex cradled her cup of coffee and didn't say anything. He wondered what she was thinking. Whatever it was, he doubted that he'd come out much of a hero. Time to change the subject.

"So what about your sordid past?" he asked teasingly. "How many hearts have you broken?"

The mug she cradled in her hands suddenly seemed to capture her attention. "Not as many as you might think," she said, all the while staring into her coffee.

"I know that's not true. A beautiful princess such as yourself must have had dozens of rich, eligible young men interested."

She shrugged, still not looking at him. "I never had much opportunity to date, at least not in the way you understand the process."

"The process? We're talking about people getting together here, not battle plans for invading an enemy nation." He leaned toward her. "I know what you're hiding. You're secretly embarrassed because you had a wild fling with the horse trainer. Come on. Admit it."

She finally raised her head and looked at him. Color stained her cheeks. "I assure you that's not the case at all. I have always planned to marry for the betterment of the kingdom. When my parents arrange an appropriate match for me, I will become engaged."

"You're kidding," he said, unable to believe what she'd told him. "Are you telling me that in this day and age you'd seriously consider an arranged marriage?"

"Of course. I'm the oldest daughter of the king of

Wynborough. I have a duty to my people and my country.''

He couldn't have been more shocked if she'd told him she'd once been a stripper at a nightclub by the airport. An arranged marriage out of duty? ''Am I ever glad I'm not part of your family,'' he muttered. ''Next you'll be telling me that you're still a virgin.''

Color climbed Alex's face, starting at her neck and spreading up to her hairline. She straightened and cleared her throat. ''My personal life is none of your business.''

He felt sucker punched. Alex a virgin? His mind reeled at the thought. While she looked younger, he knew that she was twenty-nine. No. That wasn't possible. She had to have—

Then the truth struck him. Of course, he thought with some relief, she was embarrassed because she *wasn't* a virgin. Talk about a tough gig. Where exactly did the local princess go when she wanted to have a good time? Mitch didn't envy her that, nor would he have wanted to be the first guy to do the wild thing with royalty. Talk about a lot of responsibility.

He realized then that they had both been silent for several minutes. He cleared his throat.

''It's getting late,'' he said.

''You're right.'' She set her mug on the coffee table. ''I should be heading off to bed.''

''Uh, yeah.'' He stood up, but all he could think about was what Alex had just said. Bed. As in her bed. As her *in* her bed. What exactly did she wear there? Was her hair loose across the pillow, or did she braid it so it wouldn't tangle in the night?

He had a sudden image of the two of them tangling in a very different way, arms and legs clasping and releasing while his fingers stroked her face, and his mouth—

"Thank you for sharing your family history with me," she said as she rose to her feet. "The album was very special."

"You're welcome."

He told himself to think about something else, that it was probably against the law to imagine a royal princess naked. But he couldn't help himself. Unfortunately, she wasn't just beautiful and elegant. She was also smart and bold and bossy as hell and he wouldn't change one thing about her. She challenged him. How was he supposed to resist that? Except he had to. Alex was many things, but she wasn't for him.

She started for the hallway. When he didn't follow, she paused and looked back at him. "Are you staying up?"

"Just for a little while. I still have some work."

"Did I keep you from that? I didn't mean to."

"You didn't keep me. I wanted to have dinner with you."

She smiled that slow, welcoming smile that sucked the strength from his legs and sent heat flooding to his groin.

"I enjoyed it, as well."

Her soft accent drove him crazy. He took a step toward her, then another. Even though he knew he shouldn't. Even though what he was thinking was wrong. He told himself to stop it. He told himself she would be offended. He told himself that it might start an international incident and—

And he couldn't take his eyes off her perfect mouth.

They were only a couple of feet apart. There wasn't much light in this part of the room, so he couldn't see her expression too clearly, nor could he guess what she was thinking. He figured the worst that would happen was that she would slap him.

"I've never kissed royalty. Do you do it differently from regular people?"

She flushed again, but didn't move away. If anything, her body seemed to sway toward his. "I don't believe so. I've never kissed a cowboy. Do *you* do it differently?"

"Most of us practice on our horses, so our women have to stomp their feet a couple of times to get us going."

"Really? I had no idea." She took a tiny step toward him.

"Sure. It works every time." He took a step toward her. Suddenly there wasn't any room between them. "I thought you were going to bed," he said.

"I thought you were going to work in your office."

"I think I'd rather kiss you."

Her blue eyes widened slightly, but she didn't turn away. Instead, slowly, deliberately, she stomped her foot.

Chapter Six

Mitch couldn't believe that the incredibly beautiful, incredibly royal Princess Alexandra had just issued an invitation for him to kiss her. He was many things, but he wasn't a man to pass up a once-in-a-lifetime opportunity. He slipped his arms around her waist and drew her even closer, until their bodies touched from shoulder to thigh. She was tall and slender, yet curvy. He could feel her breasts flattening against his chest in a way that would keep him hard for days. Soft curls framed her face, and the last thing he saw before he closed his eyes and pressed his mouth to hers was her expression of startled desire.

He half expected her to pull away and stop things before they had much of a chance to begin. But she didn't. Instead, she stayed very still as he moved his lips against hers. She smelled sweet and womanly.

Her lips were soft and yielding, and when she shuddered slightly in his embrace, it was all he could do not to plunge his tongue inside her mouth and tease her until she was breathless.

He'd expected the wanting, and it didn't disappoint him. The tension in his body increased as blood pumped hotter and faster. His groin ached. Then she placed her hands on his shoulders and parted her mouth. Two small acts that shouldn't have meant a damn thing, except maybe that she didn't dislike him kissing her. But her acceptance and her invitation combined to ignite a fire inside of him he'd never felt before. Desire, need, hunger—whatever it was called—slammed into him and through him, leaving him gasping for air. Instead of just wanting to deepen the kiss, he found himself wanting to shove her up against a wall and do it with them both standing up. He'd been blindsided, and he didn't even know what had hit him. Worse, he hadn't even really kissed her.

But even as he gently stroked her lower lip with his tongue, then slipped inside her mouth, he knew how it was going to be. Pure perfection brought on by a combination of chemistry, timing and maybe some dumb luck thrown in for good measure. This was more than getting turned on, he thought in shock. This was a summer thunderstorm, all heat and light and sweet darkness. He wanted to get lost inside of Alex and never find his way out.

As he touched his tongue to hers, he felt the fire lick across his skin. She tasted right, she felt right in his arms. Her body, oh, Lord, what she was doing to him. And she wasn't even trying. She was just standing there, her arms wrapped around his neck. What would happen if she actually touched him? He got harder at the thought, harder and more aroused. He tried telling himself it was just a kiss, but that was sort of like calling the Grand Canyon just a hole in the ground.

Alex found it difficult to breathe. At first she'd encouraged Mitch to kiss her because, well, no one had wanted to in a long time. He was a decent man. Good-looking, hardworking and honest. He made her laugh. Best of all, he didn't treat her as though she was different. Around Mitch she could occasionally forget she was a princess and instead pretend to be just a regular woman. Besides, when he'd looked at her with something she nearly dared to call desire, he'd made her insides go all squishy. So she'd allowed herself to cross the line just a little and kiss him.

But this wasn't a kiss, she thought hazily as large, strong male hands stroked up and down her back. She'd been kissed a few times in the past, and those embraces had been nothing like this. She remembered feeling pleasantly aroused and warm and even a little wicked. But in Mitch's arms, she found herself practically squirming. Her legs trembled, her breasts ached, and she could feel her panties getting wet. Worse, she wanted to rub herself against him like a cat. She wanted him to touch her…everywhere.

He plunged inside her mouth again. She circled around him, tasting him, caressing him, holding back the moan of pleasure that formed at the back of her throat. She wanted this. She wanted more.

When his hands dropped to her rear, she gasped. He squeezed her curves and drew her closer. Her belly pressed against something hard. His...his... Oh, my.

Alex drew back and stared at him. In all her twenty-nine years she'd never made love before. She'd known that she would have to make a political marriage for the sake of her country and she'd always thought it was important for her to save herself for her future husband. None of the men she'd ever dated had pushed for intimacy, and she'd found it surprisingly easy to avoid sexual entanglements. In fact, she'd never seen a naked man or felt an erection, even through clothing.

Mitch didn't seem to notice her surprise, or her withdrawal. He cupped her face in his large, competent hands and stared at her. "You're so beautiful," he murmured. "And one amazing kisser." A smile tugged at the corners of his mouth. "I'm impressed, princess. You've got me all hot and bothered."

He pressed his mouth to her forehead, then her nose, her cheeks and finally trailed damp kisses down her neck. Shivers rippled through her. She could only cling to him and pray that he would never stop what he was doing. How could she, an inexperienced, sexually unaware woman, have turned on someone like him? The thought thrilled her and gave her a sense of feminine power that she'd never before experienced.

She tested her newfound ability by touching his

chin and drawing his mouth back to hers. "Tell me about being hot and bothered," she murmured.

He swore under his breath, right before he claimed her mouth. This time when he hauled her up against him there was no mistaking his need. It flexed against her belly in a way that made her thighs start to melt. She wanted him. She, Princess Alexandra of Wynborough, actually wanted to make love with a man so desperately she didn't care about anything else. She wanted to throw caution to the wind and experience what it was most other women took for granted. She wanted to be naked and vulnerable and—

Reality crashed in on Alex. For one brief second she saw herself as if she were an observer of the situation instead of a participant. She saw herself as if this moment had been captured by a tabloid photographer and plastered across every newspaper in the world. Despite her desire, despite how much she liked Mitch, she wasn't a regular woman and this wasn't a normal situation.

She broke away from him. "I can't," she whispered. Even though she wanted to. Perhaps even *because* she wanted to. She looked at Mitch. "It's not you, it's me."

She thought he might protest or ask for an explanation. Instead, she read understanding in his eyes. "I'm sorry," he said. "I shouldn't have—"

"Don't apologize," she told him. "I'm glad we..." She made a vague gesture with her hand. Then she shrugged. "I just can't."

They stood less than a foot apart, staring at each other. The silence turned awkward, and when she

couldn't think of a single thing to say to him, Alex
walked out of the room.

Shortly after three in the morning, Alex gave up
trying to sleep. She figured she might as well get
started on her day. But instead of getting up and
dressing, she found herself reliving the magic of
Mitch's kiss. For the thousandth time. She closed her
eyes and imagined herself back in his arms. She could
inhale his scent, taste his sweetness on her tongue
and, most amazing of all, she could feel his need
pressing against her.

When she found herself squirming in bed, she
opened her eyes and sat up. What was it about his
kisses that had made such an impact on her? Why
him and why not some other man? Was it their circumstances and the fact that they'd been thrown together? Was it some chemical thing? A combination
of hormones and timing? Was it that he saw her as a
woman rather than a princess?

"It doesn't matter," she said aloud into the darkness. For some reason, kissing Mitch had been different from kissing other men. While the news was
potentially interesting, it didn't have to mean anything. It had been one kiss, or at least one series of
kisses. No harm had been done. She was in Arizona,
trying to find out about her long-lost brother. Mitch
had been a momentary distraction. They had kissed.
Now they simply had to put the experience behind
them.

She flopped back on the bed and pulled the covers
up to her chin. Except she couldn't stop thinking

about what they'd done. Even as she gave herself the lecture about being sensible, half her brain was caught up in the memory of his hands touching her rear. She stifled a giggle. No man had ever touched her there, yet Mitch hadn't even hesitated. He'd just reached down and squeezed. If she hadn't stopped him, he might have touched her in other, more interesting places.

Instead of the thought appalling her, she found herself wondering what it would have felt like. Would he have taken her dress off? Would he have touched her breasts? The image left her breathless.

"Stop being a fool," she told herself, trying to be stern. "He's not for you."

And he wasn't. The thing was, she'd never really thought of herself as the passionate type. Except, in Mitch's arms she'd certainly been passionate and willing. So what was different? Was it him? Or her? Or both?

Did it matter? She couldn't pursue anything with Mitch. She was the oldest daughter of a king, and he was a rancher. Her life was in Wynborough and his was in Arizona. Even if she wanted a relationship with Mitch, it wasn't possible. Besides, would he want more than just sex with her?

"I just won't think about it," she said firmly. "I will put the kiss and all it implies out of my mind. I will pretend it never happened. I'm sure Mitch will do the same. We'll go on as before. Nothing has changed."

That decided, Alex turned on her side. She would make one more attempt at sleep. But instead of growing drowsy, once again she found herself caught up in the memories of the magic that had been Mitch's kiss.

Two days later when Alex walked into the barn in the early afternoon, she was shocked to see Mitch standing in front of one of the stalls. She hadn't seen him since the night of their kiss. That next morning, after she'd slept until nearly ten, which was startling in and of itself, she'd found that she was on her own. Betty had informed her that Mitch had left shortly after dawn to buy a mare he'd been interested in for some time.

Alex had tried not to take the news personally and after sternly lecturing herself two or three more times, she'd actually been able to put him and their kiss out of her mind. She'd spent the last two days working in her office in the morning, then out in the barn in the afternoon. She'd only thought about Mitch every ten or fifteen minutes and the kiss maybe half as many times.

But now he was here, and all the physical sensations and emotional confusion crashed in on her. She didn't know if she should announce her presence or make a strategic retreat. Before she could decide, he glanced up and saw her.

"Come meet the new lady in my life," he said, motioning her forward.

Alex walked over to the stall and saw a beautiful bay mare. But instead of moving toward her visitors, the animal shuddered and backed into a corner.

Mitch's expression tightened. "She's one of the

best brood mares I've ever run across. I tried to buy her three years ago, but the owner sold him to a neighbor. Unfortunately that particular bastard isn't known for treating horses well. He's got her so spooked, she hasn't foaled in eighteen months. I finally convinced him to sell her to me.''

He turned his attention back to the mare. ''Come on, sweet thing. You're going to be happy here.'' The mare flattened her ears and bumped into the corner.

Mitch moved back a couple of steps. ''Her offspring are prizewinners, but it's going to take a lot of time to get her relaxed enough to breed again.''

Alex didn't know what to say. She was torn between responding to his conversation about the mare and wondering how he could act so...so...normal. Then she reminded herself that their kiss might have only been significant to her. Maybe Mitch felt that kind of passion all the time.

''You'll never guess her name,'' he said, studying the mare rather than her.

She was too caught up in her reaction to him to come up with even one creative response. ''What is it?''

He shot her a grin. ''Princess.'' Then he held up his hands. ''Before you say anything, I swear I didn't make that up or change it because of you. I can show you her papers if you'd like.''

''No. I believe you.'' She pushed up the sleeves of her light jacket and studied the mare. ''She's very beautiful.''

''I thought maybe you'd like to try working with her.''

She glanced at Mitch in surprise. "Me?"

"Sure." He smiled. "You're patient and gentle, not to mention female. Most of her abuse came from high-handed males. You're good with horses, and I trust you, Alex."

A thrill of pleasure zipped through her, but this wasn't the passionate kind. This warmth came from his praise and the fact that he'd noticed her work. "I'd like that," she told him sincerely. She gestured to the large barn. "I know that I've been an intrusion on your life, but I want to thank you again for putting up with me. I'm really enjoying my time here."

"Not too quiet?"

"Not at all. I love the peace and the silence." She leaned against the stall door. "It's not that I mind the visitors who are always touring the castle. I understand that their interest is important to the continuation of the monarchy. On a practical level, the money they bring in helps defray the cost of upkeep on a very old building." She paused. "But sometimes I wish home could just be home."

Mitch folded his arms over his chest. "Tourists? In the castle?"

"We do tours. Similar to what is offered at your White House." She smiled. "I confess I also don't miss the servants."

"You don't mind turning down your own bed?"

She made a show of glancing over her shoulder. "Don't tell anyone, but just yesterday Betty showed me how to use the washer. I actually did my own laundry."

He grinned. "Hey, that's more than I do."

"So she said." She looked at him, at his handsome face and the way his smile made his eyes scrunch up at the corners. "My point is, I appreciate the opportunity to be here, even for a short period of time. It's been very restful."

Mitch nodded thoughtfully. "I know what you mean. When I was on the rodeo circuit, I used to get homesick. I didn't like going to a different town every weekend. All the crowds, the strange beds."

"I've seen rodeos on television. It's a difficult sport. Did you get hurt?"

He shrugged. "I broke a few bones, but that's it. I was young and I thought I wanted the adventure." His smile returned. "And the women."

"Rodeo groupies? Like the rock stars have?"

"Similar. We call 'em buckle bunnies."

She frowned and tried to remember where she'd heard that expression before. "Oh. You called me that when I first arrived. You thought that was why I was here. Because I wanted to, well…" Her voice trailed off. She felt the heat on her cheeks and had to turn away to study the quiet bay mare standing in the center of her stall.

"Speaking of which."

Mitch's voice came from much closer than it had, just a moment before. When she turned back to him, she found that he'd moved next to her. He wore jeans and a faded blue shirt, but she didn't care about that. He had a strength about him. Being with Mitch made her feel more safe than any number of royal bodyguards.

"About that kiss," he said.

Alex had to swallow before she could speak. "Oh, that." She wanted to look away, but she didn't want him to know how much she'd been affected by their embrace. She kept her gaze on his face. "What did you want to say?"

"I'm not sorry it happened." He reached out his hand as if he was going to touch her face, then he lowered his arm to his side. "But it would never work out between us. Sex, I mean. It would be great. But it would complicate things. Neither of us wants that."

"You're right. Neither of us does." Her voice was steady, despite the trembling of her legs and the rapid flutter of her heart. He thought the sex would be great? It was all she could do to keep herself from grinning or asking how he could be so sure. Not that she doubted him or wanted him to believe otherwise.

"So my suggestion is that we pretend it never happened."

She nodded sagely. "Of course. It's already forgotten."

"We'll just be friends."

"Yes. Friends would be wise."

But he was standing terribly close for a man who was just her friend, she thought as heat from his body seeped into hers. And there was a glint of something in his brown eyes. Wanting, maybe? Desire? Her stomach had started tightening at the thought of him so near to her, and her legs weren't getting any steadier. There was also the issue of her mouth which seemed to be quivering ever so slightly.

"Speaking of friends...and family," she said, making an effort to sound casual. "Have you heard from your brother?"

"Not yet."

They stared at each other. Mitch started to lean toward her, then straightened, turned on his heel and headed for the door.

"I gotta make a call," he yelled over his shoulder.

But his rapid retreat didn't fool her for a second. Mitch Colton wanted her. Alex felt it all the way to her bones. What a heady feeling to know that a handsome, virile man wanted her in his bed. No one had before. She didn't doubt that there had been many men interested in her, but much more for the power and prestige she would bring rather than for herself. Mitch didn't care that she was a princess. If anything, her lineage was a complication he didn't want.

She turned to the mare with the bruised expression. "This is all probably very strange to you," she murmured as she reached in her pocket and pulled out a sliced apple. She held a piece in the palm of her hand. "Humans and their odd rituals. Your way is much more sensible. It's about biology and one's place in the herd."

The mare took a tentative step closer. Her gaze had settled on the slice of apple.

"The problem is, I don't know my place," Alex admitted, keeping her voice low and gentle. She knew it didn't matter what she said, she just had to keep talking. Winning the animal's trust was going to take time and patience.

"You're going to like it here," she continued. "Mitch is a fine man. Very gentle. He won't let anyone hurt you. In time you'll feel better and you'll be able to have lots of pretty babies. Won't that be nice?''

Alex ignored the familiar ache inside of her, the one that reminded her how much she wanted to be a mother, too. A dream she rarely allowed herself. When had life gotten so complicated?

The mare shied suddenly and returned to the corner of the stall. Alex put the slice of apple on the top of the door and took several steps back. Nearly a full five minutes later, the mare approached and snatched away the treat. At that moment Alex knew the mare was going to be fine. It would take a while, but the animal would heal, and her trust in people would be restored.

As Alex walked out of the barn, she wished she could be as sure about her own outcome. There were so many unanswered questions. What if they found her brother? What if they didn't? The laws of Wynborough required that a male heir inherit the throne, but without her brother, there were no male heirs.

What about her? What did she want? As she stepped into the cool afternoon light, she caught sight of Mitch driving out to check on the cattle. Her heart stirred in her chest, and her breath caught in her throat. Mitch? Did she want him? But she was a princess and he was a rancher, and there was no way to make their two worlds intersect. She had a duty to her country and to her parents. And Mitch, what did he have? She looked at the well-kept barn, the low, one-story ranch house and the mountains in the distance. Mitch, she decided, had the most perfect life imaginable.

Chapter Seven

Mitch leaned back in his leather chair in the living room and sipped from his mug of coffee. It was nearly seven on Sunday evening, which meant that Alex had been living at the ranch for a week. While it was strange having her in the house, it was also strange to think about the fact that her time was temporary. Once he'd made an effort to get to know her, he'd found that he liked her. Who would have thought that possible?

The phone rang just as the grandfather clock struck the hour. As always, his parents were right on time.

"Mitch," they said together when he picked up the receiver.

"Mom, Dad. How are you two?"

"We're fine," his mother said. "It's been gray and cool almost every day. I'm still having trouble adjusting to these northwest winters. I miss the sunshine.''

Mitch listened with half an ear. He'd already made the decision not to tell them about Alex. Even though they'd been cleared by security and he knew he could trust them to keep the information to themselves, he'd figured that explaining about a princess on the premises was going to be complicated. Plus, he wasn't sure how they would feel at the thought of John meeting his birth parents, assuming he was Alex's long-lost brother. Better to let things take their natural course. If John was Alex's brother, there would be time enough for explanations later. If he wasn't, there was no reason for his parents to be concerned.

''We're completely booked for the holidays,'' his mother was saying. ''Most of the people have been with us before. Now, I know it's hard for you to get away, but your father and I would both like to see you.''

''I know, Mom,'' he hedged as he heard footsteps in the hallway. He'd gone up to see his folks at the holidays a few times since they'd moved, but this year he wasn't so sure. Would Alex still be around? Would she be heading back to Wynborough?

''Promise us you'll think about it,'' his father told him.

''I'll give it a lot of thought.''

He looked up as Alex walked into the room. On cue, his heart rate increased, as did his blood pressure. He could feel the heat filling his body, settling in different places, before moving on again. Whatever attraction he'd felt for her before had only multiplied since he'd kissed her. Now when his overactive imagination flashed images of him with Alex, he had more details to make it real. He knew how her body felt pressed against his. He knew her taste and her scent and the way her breath would catch in her throat when he ran his hands up and down her spine. He knew that she started out a little shy when she kissed, but after she got into it she was wild and passionate and made him want in ways he'd never wanted before.

She smiled at him and showed him a pack of cards. "I thought you might enjoy being humiliated at poker," she said. "I know several rather amazing games, some of which—" Her gaze settled on the receiver pressed against his ear and she quickly mouthed an apology.

But it was already too late. He heard a soft sound from the other end of the phone and knew that his parents had heard the female voice.

"You have company," his mother said, her voice bright with excitement. "Who is she?"

"Doesn't matter who she is," his dad announced. "Mitch, you finally went out and found yourself another woman. Good for you. I'm sure we'll like her very much."

Alex had moved to the sofa and taken a seat. She looked beautiful in an elegant dark green dress that more than hinted at the curves it concealed. She'd piled her hair on top of her head, leaving only a few curls to tumble down to her shoulders. She looked regal and unapproachable.

"It's not what you think," he said quickly into the

phone. "Alex is a friend and nothing more. She's in the area, looking for relatives."

"Do we know her?" his mother asked. "What relatives? Was she adopted like John?"

"Not exactly." He hesitated, not wanting to tell them too much.

"Is she pretty?" This question came from his dad. "I guess it doesn't matter *why* she's visiting, as long as you take advantage of the situation."

"Robert! I can't believe you said that to our son. Mitch is a gentleman. He would never take advantage of a young woman."

"I didn't say for him to take advantage of *her*. I said the situation. The ranch can be a real romantic place."

Alex motioned for him to cover the mouthpiece, which he did.

"I'm sorry I started talking without noticing you were on a phone call," she said quietly. "Now that they know I'm here, you might as well tell them the truth. Otherwise, they're going to assume you're keeping a woman here."

"Too late for that one," he said. "Are you sure you don't mind?"

"They're your family, Mitch," she answered, as if that explained everything.

He returned his attention to the call and found his parents were still quarreling. "It's a nonissue," Mitch said. "Yes, she's very pretty, but she's also Princess Alexandra of Wynborough. You've probably seen several pieces about her and her sisters on the news.

The four princesses are here in America to publicize their father's upcoming celebration.''

There was a moment of stunned silence from the other end of the phone. ''A princess?'' his mother asked. ''In our house?''

''Yeah.'' He winked at Alex. ''Hard to believe, huh? She's really nice. Almost like a regular person. I have her helping me with the horses.''

''Mitch, you don't!''

''Not cleaning out the stables, but she is exercising some of the mares. Don't worry, Mom, she likes it.''

Alex nodded in agreement. ''Tell her that her house is lovely.''

''Alex says to tell you that she thinks the house is lovely.''

''You call her Alex?'' His mother sounded as if she were in shock.

''I do, but Betty uses her whole title.'' He hesitated. ''It's okay that you two know about her being here, but you can't tell anyone. She's in the area looking for relatives, and she doesn't want the press finding out that she's here. To be honest, neither do I. The last thing the cattle or the horses need are to be invaded by news vans and helicopters.''

''We won't say a word,'' his father promised, then chuckled. ''Well, I'll be. A real princess, just like on television.''

''Mitch?'' His mother cleared her throat. ''Tell Betty to use the good china when she serves dinner, and be sure to take a couple of photos for the family album.''

"I'll do that," he promised. They chatted for a couple more minutes, then hung up.

Alex raised her eyebrows. "Let me guess. They were in shock."

"Actually, they took it pretty well. Mom wants me to take your picture so we can put it in the family album."

"Then I would be part of your history." She tucked a loose curl behind her ear. "I believe I like that idea. We'll have to plan it so that you can see I'm actually in the house." She flashed him a smile. "It will make her bragging rights so much better."

"Thanks for understanding about my folks. They won't tell anyone."

"I know. I trust them. After all, look what a great job they did with their son."

Her praise made him both proud and uncomfortable. To change the subject he pointed to the deck of cards in her hand. "Still up to getting your fanny whipped at poker?"

"Absolutely, although I should warn you I'm something of a card shark."

"Yeah, right."

She rose to her feet and laughed. "You'll see. In a matter of a few hands, I'll have you begging for mercy."

He followed her into the dining room. They took seats across from each other. She opened the package of cards, then shuffled them expertly. Mitch eyed her flying fingers and realized she might not have been kidding about her abilities.

"We'll start with something simple," she said as

she dealt the cards. "Five card draw, one-eyed jacks wild. Oh, and Mitch? I want to head over to The Sunshine Home tomorrow. I've heard back from the owner and they're finally ready to let me go through their old records."

He studied his hand. Two ladies and a pair of fives. Not bad. "If you can wait until the afternoon, I'll go with you." He passed her his lone three, facedown.

"You don't have to do that."

She dealt him another card. A third five. He had to hold back his grin of pleasure.

"I don't want you going alone." When she gave him a questioning glance, he shrugged. "I know, it's a little town and nothing is going to happen. But I would feel better if you weren't by yourself. Besides, with the two of us there, the work will go faster."

"Thanks. I appreciate that. Your help will be welcome." She spread her cards on the table. "Three tens."

He tossed his hand down. "Full house."

When she pressed her lips together in minor irritation, he laughed. "Could be worse, princess. This way you're only losing money, but if I'd set the rules of the game, you'd be taking off that dress right about now."

She looked at him calmly. "Strip poker?"

"Game?"

"Why don't you see how the next few hands go. Then you can ask me that question again."

"I can't believe how much money you won from me," Mitch grumbled the next afternoon as they drove into the parking lot of The Sunshine Home.

"*I* can't believe you're still complaining," Alex told him good-naturedly. "I warned you that I was very good."

"But I won the first three games."

"It takes me a while to warm up." She tried to control her expression so he couldn't tell she was secretly gloating. "Now aren't you glad we didn't play strip poker? That chair would have been very cold on your bare bottom."

"You're forgetting you lost the first three hands. I might have been the first one to get naked, but you would have had to undress some yourself."

"Shoes and earrings," she said as she stepped out of his car. "Actually, just one earring. After all, I only lost three games."

"That's cheating," Mitch complained.

"No, it's sensible."

He muttered something she couldn't hear and led the way to the front of The Sunshine Home. She smiled at him as he held the door open for her to allow her to enter first. "And here I thought you'd be a gracious loser."

"I'm gracious about many things, but not that, princess."

"Want a rematch?"

"Maybe."

They were, she realized with a start, flirting. She wasn't sure she'd ever allowed herself to flirt with a man before. There were so many times when she had to be careful, so that a casual remark wasn't misunderstood. Her belief that she would marry for the good of her country had kept her from forming close friendships with many men. To make the problem even more complicated, very few men felt comfortable just being themselves around her. Mitch was a rare and very special man. She was fortunate to have met him.

Twenty minutes later, she was even more grateful. As she surveyed the large, dusty storage room with its piles of boxes, her stomach sank. "This could take weeks," she said as she read the different labels indicating the types of information stored inside.

Mitch looked around at the hundreds of files and records. "You're probably not going to find out what you want today," he admitted. "They weren't kidding when they said they hadn't gotten everything on the data base. At least they had the boxes delivered here so you didn't have to dig around in the various storage facilities they'd been renting. One place is easier than three." He shook his head at the mess. "Tell you what. Let me get the files in order so they'll be easier for you to go through." He flexed an arm. "Might as well take advantage of the muscle while it's here."

Alex looked at the tall stacks. There had to be over a hundred boxes. "I'll help," she said, motioning to her jeans and long-sleeve shirt. "I dressed to get grubby. Besides, it will go faster if we do this together."

"Works for me."

Mitch started clearing a space against the far wall. Alex picked up a box and read the label. "I suppose we should sort them by year. If we put all the ones that won't help on one side of the room, that will cut down what I have to look through.''

''You're the boss.''

While she carried boxes one at a time, Mitch picked up two or three each time he crossed the room. Unfortunately some of the containers had five or ten years' worth of records, so the sorting wasn't going to help all that much. But it was a start.

As she worked, Alex wrestled with her conflicting emotions. The longer the job took, the more time she could spend at the ranch. In the past week she'd relaxed enough to enjoy the quiet and the rhythm of her days. She wasn't so sure she wanted to get back to her regular life. The thought of hectic, event-filled afternoons and evenings, not to mention official functions, made her cringe. Until she'd had the chance to live without the constant scrutiny of her family, servants and the public, she hadn't realized how high a price she'd paid to always be on her guard.

Unfortunately, Alex wasn't sure what to make of the revelation. Shouldn't she be anxious to get back to her regular life? Shouldn't she miss the palace, her family and her duties? She drew in a deep breath. In some ways she *did* miss her normal contact with her sisters and her parents, although they spoke daily by phone. But she would have expected to feel more out of place on Mitch's ranch.

''Here's something,'' Mitch said.

She glanced up and saw him crouch down as he raised a lid on one of the boxes. ''What is it?''

''I happened to notice the label when I set the box

down,'' he told her. ''These are lists of the children adopted the same year as John. Now it might not say when they arrived, but it's a start.''

She knelt next to him on the floor and took the files he handed her. They both scanned the labels on the aging and dusty manila folders. There were dozens of names.

''I had no idea there were going to be so many children adopted from here,'' Alex said.

Mitch opened a couple of folders. ''The good news is you can eliminate all the girls, not to mention the boys who are too old. That will cut the number down.''

''Not by enough.'' Alex studied a file. ''Here it lists a child's age as anywhere from eleven to sixteen months. They're guessing, which means we have to broaden the age range we're looking at. So it would have to be boys under the age of two.''

He looked at her, his brown eyes dark with concern. ''Are you discouraged already?''

''Not really, but I did have the unrealistic expectation that this would be a lot easier. Foolish of me, I suppose. It's not as if the police or royal security detail were able to find James, and they're trained professionals. What shot do we have?''

''They didn't know about The Sunshine Home,'' Mitch reminded her. ''Don't forget about the baby blanket. That has to mean something.''

''You're right.''

She continued to flip through files, sorting them into different piles. Those to investigate, those that were unlikely candidates and finally those that didn't fit at all. She glanced at the remaining boxes and wondered how many more records would need to be studied. The task was daunting.

Mitch gave a low whistle. "Well, I'll be. Who'd have known?"

"What are you talking about?"

He thrust an open folder toward her. "I know this guy. Bill Lewis. He went to school with John. They were friends. But I never knew that Bill had been here, too. He came in the same year your brother disappeared. Looks like a month after the fire. He was adopted shortly after that." He tapped the folder. "If you're missing a prince, you need to take a look at this guy."

She took the folder from him and studied the loose pages inside. "Why do you say that?"

Mitch raised his eyebrows. "You haven't heard of Bill Lewis?" When she shook her head, he continued. "He's an incredibly wealthy businessman. Self-made. He's been on the cover of dozens of business magazines. He's got the Midas touch and then some." Mitch's gaze narrowed. "I can't tell if he looks anything like you, but there are enough similarities that it's worth checking into."

Alex reached for her purse and pulled out her cell phone. She dialed the number of the Aspen house from memory, then asked to speak with Katherine.

"We've found something," Alex said when her sister came to the phone.

"About James?" Katherine asked.

"I think so. I'm at The Sunshine Home, going through old records. There was one child brought in shortly after our brother disappeared. His name is Bill Lewis. Apparently he's a very successful business-man.''

''All right. What do you think we should do?''

Alex hesitated. ''Investigate. Is Elizabeth still…'' Her voice trailed off.

On the other end of the phone Katherine sighed. ''Acting strange? Yes. I'm not sure why. I've tried speaking with her, but she won't say if anything's wrong. I talked with Serena, but you know how she is. Why do you ask?''

''Someone has to look into Bill Lewis, and obvi-ously you're the only one who can do that. I hate for you to go alone, but Serena would just be trouble, and with Elizabeth not herself I don't see another choice.''

''I'll be fine,'' Katherine promised. ''You're sur-viving by yourself. Why should it be different for me?''

Alex didn't know how to answer that. She'd always seen herself as more independent than her sisters. That probably came from being the oldest. No doubt they would tell her it was because she was bossy and insisted on getting her way.

''I know you'll do well. Just be careful and stay in touch every day.''

''I will. I guess this means you don't have any news about John Colton.''

''Not yet,'' Alex admitted. ''Mitch has talked to his parents, and they'll let him know if John contacts them. In the meantime, all I can do is wait—'' she glanced around the room ''—and go through these records. There are dozens of boxes. I might need Elizabeth and Serena to come help.''

''Just say the word. They'll be there.''

''Thanks. I'll do some more on my own and see how far I get.''

Alex shared the details about Bill Lewis that Mitch had provided, then she hung up.

''That guy won't know what hit him,'' Mitch said with a grin. ''I know I didn't. How often does a regular guy meet a real live Princess?'' He kicked the closed box with the toe of his boot. ''Ready to get back to the salt mines?''

''If that means am I ready to look through more files, certainly.''

They worked until it was dark. The single bulb in the room didn't give off much light, and when Mitch suggested they stop for the day, Alex agreed. ''I'll make time to come back later in the week,'' she said.

She glanced up and saw Mitch staring at her. He had the oddest expression on his face, and she couldn't help reaching up and brushing her fingers against her cheek. ''Am I smudgy?''

He grinned. ''Nope. I was just wondering. It's getting late and I'm hungry.''

Alex's stomach growled in response to his statement. She laughed. ''I guess I am, too.''

''So we can head back to the ranch and eat there, or we can eat here, in town. The local diner has great food, if Her Highness doesn't mind dining with the little people.''

''I've never eaten at a diner,'' she admitted. ''That

sounds like fun. And I promise not to make anyone bow unless he or she wants to.''

It wasn't a date, Alex told herself firmly, but it was too late. Her heart had already started thundering in her chest, and she could feel her thighs getting weak.

Dinner out with Mitch. If it wasn't a date, it was close enough to make her wish the evening would never end.

Chapter Eight

"This was my favorite place to come for dinner when I was a kid," Mitch said as he held open the door to Ruby's Diner. He leaned close to Alex and lowered his voice. "They don't get many of the royal set, so don't expect much except good, plain food, okay? There's not going to be salmon mousse or pâté on the menu."

She glanced at him over her shoulder and smiled. "What? No pâté? Then I'll just have to stamp my royal foot in a dainty manner and demand they buy some for me."

Mitch was still grinning as he followed her into the diner. The large, brightly lit restaurant was just as he remembered. Booths lined three walls, their red vinyl seats as shiny as ever. Different-size tables filled the space between the booths and the counter seating. All the tabletops were red and gray Formica. Menus stood between metal napkin holders and bottles of mustard and ketchup. Country music blared out of the speakers, and the smell of grilled hamburgers and steaks filled the air.

Alex paused to take it all in. She'd dressed casually for their trip to The Sunshine Home, and her still-too-new jeans outlined her slender hips and long legs. She'd pulled a navy jacket over her white shirt. Her hair was back in some fancy braid, and she didn't have on much makeup. Even so, she was obviously high-class and incredibly beautiful. Mitch saw the interested glances in their direction and knew that he'd have some questions to answer.

"Sit anywhere you'd like," a female voice hollered from behind the counter. "The T-bone is better than the rib-eye tonight, and the mashed potatoes are so good they'll make you cry."

Alex pointed to a booth in front of the main window. When he nodded, she led the way over and slid onto the bench seat. "I've never cried over potatoes before," she admitted as he took a seat across from her.

"Then you'll have to try them, won't you?"

"I suppose so." She slipped off her jacket and glanced around. "I like this place. It reminds me of that movie—*American Graffiti*. The one set in the early sixties. Did you see it?"

"Many times."

"Me, too. It's a favorite of mine and my sisters." She took a menu and opened it. Her eyes widened as she took in the list of steaks and all the ways they could be cooked. "This isn't a place for a nonmeat eater, is it?"

"They have salad."

She grinned. "One salad. Amazing. And..." She paused to count. "Three dishes made with chicken. Four, if you count chicken-fried steak."

"Hey, Mitch."

He looked up and saw an older man standing next to the table. "Tom." Mitch shook the man's hand. "How's by you?"

"Good. I haven't seen you in town for a while. Keeping busy on the ranch?"

"Yeah. With my folks gone and John away, there's plenty of work to fill my day."

Tom Bucannan's spread was about five miles from Mitch's. Tom and his dad had always been friends, but unlike Mitch's father, Tom would never retire. The rancher always said he didn't see the point of leaving the one thing he'd worked for all his life. He was a tall man, strong but lean, with gray hair and a handlebar mustache that stuck out straight for nearly four inches before curving into graceful half circles. His sharp gaze settled on Alex.

Mitch drew in a deep breath. How exactly did one explain the presence of royalty at Ruby's Diner?

"Tom, this is Alex. She's a friend of the family and is staying with me for a little while. Alex, Tom Bucannan, our closest neighbor."

She gave the rancher one of her best smiles and shook hands with him. "This is such a beautiful part of the country," she said graciously. "I'm very pleased to have had the chance to see it."

Tom continued to hold her hand in his. "If you've just been around Mitch's place, you ain't seen nothing. Ride on up to my spread. I'll show you some countryside that will keep you talking for days."

"I would like that very much."

Mitch wondered if the older man was ever going to release Alex's fingers. He finally did so, then tipped his hat and left.

"We have some colorful characters up here," Mitch said by way of explanation.

"I liked him." Her blue eyes danced with amusement. "Although you were glaring."

"I was not." Tom was old enough to be her father and then some. He *hadn't* been glaring. He cleared his throat, then changed the subject. "I hope you don't mind that I introduced you as a friend of the family. I didn't think you wanted everyone knowing who you were."

"That's fine." She rested her forearms on the table. "I liked that, too. No one has ever said that about me before. Probably because no one would be comfortable with that kind of familiarity."

Mitch stiffened at her comment. He knew in his head that she was a royal princess, but with her exercising the horses and living in his house, he often forgot it on a day-to-day basis. Most of the time she was just a smart, intriguing, attractive woman who had taken up temporary residence on the ranch.

"So how many rules of etiquette have I violated in the past week and a half?" he asked.

"Nearly 750."

"I'm being serious."

Her smile faded. She reached across the table and touched the back of his hand. "Please don't be." She paused and drew in a deep breath. "You're the most genuine person I know, Mitch. You treat me like I'm very normal. My guess is that you forget the princess part, and I don't want that to change."

She pulled her hand free and leaned forward, staring at him intensely. "You can't know what it's like for me. Everywhere I go, I'm treated differently. It can be very isolating. I never have the opportunity to just be myself. I'm expected to dress a certain way or act a certain way. I'm not supposed to be irritable or too quiet or even make off-color jokes. But at the ranch, around you, I'm safe to be myself. That means the world to me."

"I hear the words, but they don't make any sense," he admitted.

"Then just accept them on faith and promise you won't change. I don't want you worrying about the rules. I want you to be yourself."

"So whatcha gonna have?" the waitress asked as she came toward the table. She was a redhead, but unlike Alex, the color of her hair was closer to neon than nature. She winked at Mitch, then turned her attention to Alex. "You made up your mind, sweetie?"

Alex looked faintly startled at the endearment, but offered a friendly smile. "Yes. I'd like the T-bone steak with mashed potatoes." She hesitated. "Is there a vegetable served with that?"

The waitress rolled her eyes toward heaven. "Of course. We serve corn with everything."

"Corn," Alex repeated softly. "Perfect."

Mitch grinned. "I'll have the same. Oh, and we'll both have blueberry milk shakes."

The waitress eyed Alex. "We might have a box of wine somewhere in the back if your lady friend would prefer that."

Boxed wine? Mitch doubted Alex would be able to choke it down. "No, the milk shake will be fine."

When the woman left, Alex laughed. "Wine in a box? I haven't heard of that before."

"It's not what you're used to."

"Neither is a blueberry milk shake, but it sounds lovely. I can't wait. Thank you for bringing me here, Mitch. I'm having a wonderful time."

Her gaze was direct, and he read the pleasure in her face. Wanting slammed into him, nearly making him wince. The situation was completely ridiculous. Here he was, a rancher from Arizona, attracted to a royal princess. They had absolutely nothing in common, they came from two different worlds, and he knew better than to get involved. There was only one problem. He liked her. It wasn't all about her long legs and pretty face. He actually enjoyed Alex's company. She made him laugh, she made him think and she didn't let him get away with anything.

So he was stuck. Liking and wanting were allowed as long as he didn't do anything about either. After all, he hadn't been able to keep his first wife happy. Of course he'd matured since then. He knew a lot more about relationships and doing his part in one. But however much he'd learned, it wasn't going to be enough to travel in royal circles.

From the corner of his eye, he caught sight of a couple walking toward them. He motioned with his head. "Little people approaching at three o'clock."

Alex looked momentarily confused, then started to laugh. "Stop teasing," she told him. "What if someone overhears?"

"They'll think you're a snob."

"That's so nice of you. Thanks. As if I don't have enough trouble in that department."

"You're the one who's bossy and imperious. I'm just a nice guy."

"You couldn't be more wrong." Her blue eyes danced as she teased him.

He opened his mouth to reply, but before he could do so, the couple had reached the side of the table.

"Mitch, it's good to see you," Reverend Tucker said as he clasped Mitch's shoulder. "You've been hiding up at the ranch for too long."

Mitch leaned toward Alex. "Translation—how come I never see you in church these days? If you don't show up soon, I'm going to call your folks in Washington and rat you out."

The reverend chuckled. "I wouldn't go that far, but it's a thought."

"I know how your mind works." He smiled at the man he'd known most of his life. "Okay, Reverend, I'll do my best to pop in some Sunday. Reverend Tucker, Mrs. Tucker, I'd like you to meet Alex. She's a friend of the family and is staying out on the ranch for a while."

"What a pretty lady," Reverend Tucker said as he

took Alex's hand. "I don't remember seeing you around here before. Is this your first trip to Hope?"

"Yes. I'm enjoying myself tremendously."

The reverend wasn't overly tall, and the years had added some weight to his medium build. Still, he carried himself with dignity. Lucy Tucker, his wife, was a prim woman, who wore her hair in a tight bun and always seemed on the verge of disapproving of whatever was going on.

"Why don't you talk this young man into bringing you to services this Sunday?" the reverend was saying. "I don't promise a lot of fancy talk, but I do stay true to the word of God."

"I would like that," Alex said.

Reverend Tucker asked her a question, but Mitch was distracted by Mrs. Tucker. The older woman stared at Alex as if she were a ghost. Lucy flushed bright red, then went pale. She placed one hand on her chest and sucked in a gasp of air.

"You're here," she said, her voice low and trembling. "I thought you looked familiar."

"What is it, dear?" Reverend Tucker asked his wife. "Are you all right?"

Lucy's gaze went from Alex to Mitch and back. "I've seen your picture on television. You're one of those princesses from that country. I know who you are!"

Her voice rose with each word until she was nearly screeching. Alex looked stunned.

"Mrs. Tucker, I—"

But Alex didn't get to finish her sentence. Lucy Tucker covered her face with her hands and ran from the restaurant. Reverend Tucker apologized quickly and hurried after his wife.

There was a moment of uncomfortable silence. Mitch felt everyone's attention focus on them, then slowly slip away. He felt almost guilty, as if he were responsible for the other woman's strange behavior.

"I'm sorry," he said.

Alex waved away his apology. "Don't be. It's not your fault. It happens."

"People get that weird on you?"

She tried to smile, but it was a little forced. "Well, they're not usually quite so overwrought, but they do get odd from time to time." She sighed. "What I hate most is the reminder that I'm not like everyone else. Just when I feel than I'm fitting in and that I can finally forget, at least for a little while, something will happen to remind me." She shrugged. "It's probably for the best."

"No, it's not," he told her. "I want you to be able to forget your past and just be a regular person. Can we pretend Lucy Tucker never stopped by the table?"

Her smile turned genuine. "That would be very nice, Mitch. Thank you."

"It's the least I can do."

She glanced around the diner. Most of the patrons had lost interest in them and their table. "It must have been fun growing up in a small town like this."

"Everyone knows everyone else and their business, which when you're a teenager isn't a good thing. As kids we had a hard time getting away with making trouble. The local sheriff always knew who was most likely to be where he wasn't supposed to be, doing things that weren't allowed.''

''How often was that person you?''

''Often enough,'' he admitted. ''I can't tell you how many times I got hauled out of Submarine Point.''

The waitress arrived with their drinks. Alex stared at the tall purple shake and wrinkled her nose. ''What is it?''

''A blueberry milk shake.''

''Somehow I thought it would be more blue than purple.'' She took a sip. ''It's good.''

''Trust me, lady, and you won't go wrong.''

''I'll trust you, but only if you tell me about Submarine Point.''

He took a long drink of his milk shake. ''It's the local make-out place. There's an overlook with a pretty decent view. We'd tell the girls that if the night was clear enough, they could see the submarines in the Pacific Ocean.''

''And they believed you?''

He grinned. ''They pretended to.''

''I suppose that was all that mattered.''

''Exactly.''

Thirty minutes later Alex pushed away her plate and patted her stomach. ''I can't believe I ate that entire steak. It had to be half a pound.''

''Probably more,'' Mitch said helpfully, ''but the bone was really big.''

''Not big enough.'' She sipped the last of her milk shake and sighed with contentment. ''I pronounce my first visit to a diner to be an unqualified success. The steak was excellent, the mashed potatoes, while not quite bringing me to tears, were certainly the best I've ever had.'' She lowered her voice. ''I think the corn came from a can, but even it wasn't too bad.''

''And you're hooked on blueberry milk shakes.''

''Absolutely.'' She glanced around at the nearly empty restaurant. ''I wish I'd had a place like this nearby when I was growing up.''

Mitch finished his last mouthful of steak, then wiped his mouth on the paper napkin. ''No Ruby's by the palace?''

''Not one.''

''Did you go to a regular school?''

''For a few years, but mostly my sisters and I had tutors. We traveled a lot as teenagers, and the tutors came with us. That allowed us to continue our studies without interruption.''

''So even as a child you attended official functions?''

''Of course.''

He shook his head. Nothing about her life made sense to him. ''I can't imagine it.''

''I can't imagine this,'' she said, motioning to the diner. ''Except now that I've been here, I'll remember it always. When the pressure of my world gets to be too much, I'll think of blueberry milk shakes and dinner with you at Ruby's.''

Her voice, with its lilting accent, still drove him crazy. But now he knew her well enough to see past the attraction to the woman inside. Her tone was light, but he heard the sadness underneath.

"When does your world get to be too much?" he asked.

"More often than I would like. There are so many responsibilities."

"Keeping the tiara on straight?" he teased.

"That, too." She hesitated. "That's what makes it so complicated about finding my brother."

"I don't understand."

"Wynborough law currently states that the heir must be male. But my parents only had one son and he's been presumed dead for years."

"What's complicated about that? Wouldn't the throne just go to the next male heir? A cousin or something?"

"It would, except there aren't any male heirs. Not without going outside the immediate family to a very distant relative. No one wants that. So there's been some talk in the palace and parliament about introducing a bill to change the law."

Mitch knew what she was going to say. It was the next logical step. But he couldn't believe it. "Change the law how?"

Alex met his gaze. "There have been proposals to make the legal heir to the throne be the oldest child, regardless of gender."

"Which would make you…" His voice trailed off.

She looked faintly uncomfortable, then raised her chin in that damn regal way she had. "That would make me queen."

Chapter Nine

Mitch felt his mouth drop open. He consciously closed it, but that didn't stop the buzzing in his head. Alex kept on talking as if she hadn't said anything out of the ordinary.

"I'm not sure if the bill would pass," she went on. "But the feeling is that it would."

He felt as if someone had just shaken his world good and hard. Only this wasn't something as insignificant as an earthquake. "Queen," he said, although the single word was tough to speak.

"Yes, similar to Queen Elizabeth of Great Britain. I can only hope I would do as good a job in leading my people. I suspect the uncertainty about the succession is one of the reasons my parents haven't pressed me to marry. If I am to be monarch of Wynborough, then my choice of husband becomes even more important.''

Mitch turned that information over in his mind. ''But he wouldn't be king.''

''Exactly.'' She shrugged. ''It would take a very special kind of man to handle the pressure of being the consort—someone married to the queen, but without any of the power. Most men would have problems being the one in the background.''

He couldn't believe they were actually having this conversation. He also couldn't believe that he hadn't really gotten it before. Alexandra was really a princess. She wasn't just some beautiful, single woman who happened to be living with him—she was royalty. She might one day rule her country.

''I can't believe I kissed you,'' he blurted out.

Her steady gaze settled on his face. ''It's too late to regret that now.''

''I don't regret it, I just hadn't realized I might be starting an international incident.''

She smiled. ''I promise I won't tell a soul.''

''You'd better not,'' he muttered, trying not to think about a half-dozen Secret Service agents bursting into the house and arresting him for having illicit thoughts about a visiting dignitary.

Alex read the confusion and panic on Mitch's face. ''Why are you suddenly so caught up in this?'' she asked. ''Nothing has changed from a few minutes ago. You've always known that I was a princess.''

He made a helpless gesture with his hands. ''Being a princess is one thing, but we're talking about your being queen. It makes a difference.''

"Not too big of one, I hope. I don't want things to change between us."

His gaze sharpened. "Why do you say that?"

"I've told you that I enjoy spending time with you on the ranch. The main reason is that I get to be a regular person. If you start thinking about me as queen of Wynborough, then everything will be different. I get enough of that in the rest of my life. I don't want it happening here, too."

His brown eyes darkened with something that might have been compassion. "I take your point," he said. "I'll admit that hearing about your potential promotion threw me a little, but I won't let it affect our relationship."

Alex had to laugh. Only Mitch would refer to her possible succession to the throne as a promotion. "Thank you. I really like being normal."

"I don't know about normal. You're a little quirky for that description. But I promise to keep treating you like regular folks." He motioned to the diner. "I brought you here, didn't I?"

"Yes, and it's been one of the highlights of my visit."

"Stick with me. I'll show you all the best sights."

"Submarine Point?" she couldn't help asking.

Mitch looked startled, then grinned. "Sure, why not."

Their waitress came by and cleared their table. "You two want coffee?" she asked.

"Please," Alex said, as Mitch nodded. When the woman returned with the steaming mugs, Alex poured cream and sugar into hers.

"So tell me about being queen," Mitch said as he cupped his mug between his hands. "Is there a class you have to take?"

"No. It's more on-the-job training. Except—" she shrugged "—it's rather confusing. In some ways my father is preparing me for eventual leadership of the country. I have more responsibility than my sisters. My father often refers to me as his right-hand girl. But I'm not given official duties that a prince would have. There are those in parliament who think a woman shouldn't rule."

"What, are they crazy? You'd do a great job."

"While I appreciate the compliment, you can't know that."

"Yes, I can. You're smart, you're capable and you're patient. More important than all that, you care. Running a country is about character, not gender."

"Very forward thinking, cowboy."

"My mama didn't raise a fool." He took a drink of coffee. "What do *you* want?"

It was a question no one ever asked her. "I don't know. If we find James, then the problem is solved."

"Do you want to find him?"

"Funny you should ask that." She tried to smile, but couldn't. "I don't know that, either. I've never met my brother, so it's not as if he was a part of my life. I don't miss him. I can't even imagine what my world would have been like if he'd been around."

"You're not answering the question."

His steady gaze didn't offer any escape. Alex supposed she could have insisted on a change of subject, but she found herself wanting to talk about this. Mitch was a neutral party, and she knew she could trust him to keep quiet.

"Sometimes I know that I would be a good queen. You're right—I do care about my country and my people. I would happily dedicate my life to them. I have many ideas about improvements. I think it's important to stay focused on the future and new opportunities while maintaining the life lessons and history of the past."

"That sounds great. But what about the other times?"

She found herself unable to meet his gaze. She stared into her mug of coffee. "Other times I'm not so sure."

"What does that mean?"

She shook her head. She couldn't say it. Not to him, not to anyone.

"Alex?"

"It's wrong and selfish."

"I don't believe that. Tell me." He stretched his arm across the table and placed his hand on top of hers.

His fingers were warm and strong as he squeezed hers. She found herself wanting to speak a truth she'd never had the courage to say aloud before. "Sometimes…sometimes I don't want to be queen, or even a princess. Sometimes I want to run away and live like everyone else. I don't want to be responsible or have to worry about the press or the country or what the people will think. Sometimes I just want to be foolish and ordinary and not think about anyone but myself."

"There's nothing wrong with that."

"Of course there is. My sisters and I have lived an extraordinary life. We've been blessed with material possessions and great responsibility. We have a warm, loving family. That should be enough. I hate that I want more. I hate that I'm not more grateful for all I've been given. I hate that I want to be like other women and just meet a man and fall in love. I hate that I'll have to worry about visiting heads of state instead of my husband, or getting back from a diplomatic trip in time to see my child's first dance recital."

I hate that I can't pick who I marry. Except she didn't say that. She could barely admit that truth to herself. But it was true. Although she'd tried very hard to be dutiful and understanding, she wanted to fall in love with the man she married. She wanted their relationship to be special, not politically sound. Sometimes her heart felt so empty and dry, she was afraid it would shatter and blow away.

"I wish I had some words of advice to offer," he said, "but I don't. I can't relate to anything you're saying. All I know is normal."

"You don't know how I envy that."

He offered her a quick smile. "I wish I could tell you that I envy you your royal life, but I don't. I've only ever wanted to live on the ranch."

"I understand why. It's beautiful there." She drew in a deep breath. "I wish…" Her voice trailed off. There was no point in wishing. Her destiny had been set a long time ago.

"You ready to go?" he asked.

When she nodded, he threw several bills on the table. Alex stared at them. "May I pay for dinner?"

"No, you may not." He helped her into her coat, then he took her elbow and led her out to the truck, muttering all the while. "Buy me dinner. That'll be the day I let a woman pay for my food. I can't believe you even asked. Talk would spread faster than wildfire if I so much as let you put down the tip. My mama didn't raise me that way."

Alex planted her heels and stared at him. "You're a sexist pig."

Instead of getting angry, Mitch grinned. "Yes, ma'am. I hold open doors, I let ladies go first and I pay for meals."

"But I'm a princess."

"I believe we've established that fact."

"No one buys me dinner."

"Then this is a first." He opened the passenger-side door for her and motioned for her to step inside. "Now if I remember correctly, little lady, you said something about wanting to go to Submarine Point."

She didn't know whether to laugh or threaten him with beheading again. "I'll get you for this," she insisted.

"I'm sure you'll try."

He waited until she was settled, then walked around to the driver's side and climbed in. As he started the truck, he squinted up at the sky. "It's nice and clear. We should be able to see all the way to the Pacific Ocean tonight."

Alex chuckled, then stopped as she had a sudden, unpleasant thought. She'd suggested going to Submarine Point in jest. Although she didn't mind seeing the view of the valley below, she didn't want Mitch thinking that she expected him to, well, do anything.

She bit back a moan. Is that what he thought? That she was demanding he kiss her or whatever it was the teenagers did up there? They'd pulled onto the two-lane highway. There weren't many other cars out on the road, and they seemed to be alone in some isolated part of the world. There was only the low sound of the engine and the faint whisper of country music coming from the truck's stereo.

"Um, Mitch?"

"Yes?"

"We don't have to go there if you don't want to. I mean, I was mostly interested in the view, and it's getting late and well, it's not necessary."

He gave her a quick glance before returning his attention to the road. "In no particular order, it's not all that late, I'm happy to show you the view and, no, you're not making me do anything I don't want to do."

Okay, so she hadn't made herself clear. It wasn't really her fault, she thought grimly. None of her etiquette classes had covered this particular situation. She was twenty-nine years old and she'd never been romantically involved with a man. It was incredibly pitiful.

"What I'm trying to say is that I have no expectations that—" She groaned low in her throat. "That didn't come out right." She tried again. "I don't expect you to feel obligated to be any way other than how you want to be."

Despite the darkness of the cab, she saw Mitch's eyebrows pull together. "You want to run that by me again?"

"Not really."

"Okay." He nodded a couple of times. "Let me see if I understand this. You're saying that your entire interest in Submarine Point is the view, and that I am under no obligation to put out. Does that about sum it up?"

If she hadn't thought it would have started an international incident, she would have thrown herself out of the cab and risked tumbling down the side of the mountain. Color heated her cheeks until she could only pray that she would die. Right there. In the truck.

"I'll take your silence for a yes," he said.

She made a low, strangled sound which he ignored.

"That leaves only one question, Princess Alexandra. Do you want me to do anything or not?"

Before she could even try to answer, he pulled the truck off the main highway and rolled onto a dirt track. They bounced along for several minutes, rounded a bend and stopped by an outcropping of rock.

Alex leaned forward and caught her breath. Lights twinkled in the valley below, while stars twinkled in the clear sky above. The darkness seemed to go on forever, but not in a way that frightened her. Instead she had the sense of being a small part of a much larger world.

"It's beautiful," she breathed.

He turned off the engine, and they were instantly surrounded by silence. Mitch opened the driver's window a couple of inches. "Pretty soon you'll be able to hear the coyotes and whatnot going about their business."

She glanced at him. "I've never seen a whatnot before. Are they indigenous to the area?"

"Mostly. Some came over with the Spanish back in the sixteen hundreds. We have several varieties of whatnot out here. The males are sturdy, loyal creatures, but the females can be a real pain in the butt."

She turned her back on him and stared out the side window. "I'm ignoring you."

"Why?"

"You're insulting me."

"For talking about whatnots?"

"You know exactly what I mean."

She pressed her lips together so that her laughter wouldn't escape. With Mitch she was able to relax more than with anyone other than her immediate family. She was both pleased and confused by that. Maybe it was their isolation on the ranch. Out here there weren't any royal rituals or reminders of who and what she was. Maybe it was the man himself. He wasn't one to stand on ceremony.

"Tell me what you're thinking," he said.

"That you make me laugh."

She spoke without turning around. Was it her or had it suddenly gotten warm in the cab? And had Mitch's voice turned low and smoky?

"I'm glad," he said. "I want you to enjoy your time on the ranch."

"I am. You're a very good host."

"Not as good as you think," he admitted.

She turned to face him and found that he'd shifted closer to the middle. Her leg bumped his knee. Her breath caught at the contact, but she couldn't find it in herself to complain…or retreat. Was it her imagination or had her breathing gotten faster? Her heart was pounding hard enough. She was afraid it might crack one or two ribs.

"What do you mean?"

"You confuse the hell out of me." In the dim light his eyes were black and bottomless. "Tonight, when you were talking about being queen of your country, I felt like I'd been kicked in the gut by a steer."

"Why? That shouldn't matter to you at all."

"Maybe not, but it does. When it's just the two of us, you're plain Alex. But then I have to remember you're much more than that. I don't know how to handle Princess Alexandra, or worse, *Queen* Alexandra."

They were both speaking softly. Alex had to force herself not to sway toward him. "I'm not a horse. I don't have to be handled."

His mouth turned up at the corners. "You know what I mean. I can't reconcile what I want with what's real."

Her heart pounded harder. "Wh-what do you want?"

Instead of answering, he reached up and, with one hand, cupped her face. His fingers were long and warm against her skin. Her eyelids drifted closed and she found herself rubbing her cheek against his palm, like a cat seeking affection.

"Tell me to take you back to the ranch," he said gruffly.

She opened her eyes and stared at him. "What?"

"Or tell me that you wanted to come out here because my kisses make you hot. That you want to pretend we're just a couple of high school kids who stole away to make out."

He was moving closer…or was it she? Not that it mattered which, she thought hazily as she licked her lips in anticipation of his kiss.

"So it's either or?" she asked. "I have to pick?"

"Yeah, but hurry up." He put his free hand on the other side of her face and held her still. "I mean it, Alex. I have to know."

She'd never done anything like this before in her life. The experience was coming about nine or ten years too late, but at least she was going to have it.

"Don't worry, Mitch," she said, her voice low and husky. "My parents aren't expecting me home for hours."

He stared at her for what felt like forever, but was actually two very loud, very excited beats of her heart.

"You are one hellcat under that bossy facade of yours," he growled, then pulled her close and kissed her.

Chapter Ten

Alex had thought about their kiss on a nearly hourly basis since it had occurred. So she should have been prepared for the impact of having Mitch kiss her again. She shouldn't have been surprised by the fire that leaped between them or the way her body seemed to melt into a needy pool of desire. But she *was* surprised by all of it. She gasped at the feel of his firm mouth against hers. His lips brushed hers, slowly at first as if he had to rediscover every curve, then faster, building tension.

Without quite being sure how, she found that she'd raised her hands to his broad shoulders and rested them there. As Mitch's tongue stroked against her bottom lip, she tensed her fingers, hanging on to him as her world started to spin.

When she parted her lips for him, his tongue

slipped into her mouth. He tasted sweet and hot and male. He explored her, his touch making her shiver with delight. They circled around each other, under and over, the rhythm making her sigh. This kiss was as good as the one she remembered. Better, maybe, because this time she wasn't so startled by the intense wanting that seemed to be flooding her. Heat flowed through her blood, igniting fires in her breasts and between her legs. She felt tension in her stomach and dampness on her panties.

She shivered with delight and a little fear. It was as if her body had been taken over by someone else. Or maybe it was because for the first time in her life, she couldn't think. She could only react and feel. Mitch was, she realized, her ultimate escape, and she never wanted to have to go back to the regular world.

"What?" he asked, pulling back slightly. "What are you thinking?"

His voice was low and husky, his breathing rough. She could feel herself struggling to fill her lungs, as well. "That when I'm with you, like this, I'm just like everyone else."

His eyebrows drew together. "I don't understand."

"Here, in the truck cab, we have our own little world. The regular rules don't apply. I don't have to worry about doing the right thing or think about my responsibilities. I can just be a normal woman."

"Is that a good thing?"

"It's magic, as are you."

He chuckled. "Princess, if anyone has any power in this situation, it's you. I'm doing all I can just to hang on and act my age."

He still cupped her face. Now he moved his thumbs against her cheeks, then across her mouth. She parted her lips and licked the salty pad. They both shuddered.

"See what I mean," he said. "You've got me so turned on that I'm about to explode. All that and we've only been kissing for five minutes. Imagine what would happen if this was a real make-out session."

"It isn't?" she asked before she could stop herself. "How disappointing."

Mitch sucked in his breath. "I can't tell if you're teasing or serious."

She wanted him to kiss her again. She wanted him to touch her and do all those things that teenagers routinely did together when they parked here at Submarine Point. Her body felt tingly and hot and tense, and she wanted more of those feelings. She wanted Mitch to hold her close and make her forget about the rest of her world. For just one night she wanted to find out what it was like to be the same as the rest of the world. For one night she wanted the magic.

"What if it's both?" she asked.

"Both is tricky," he admitted. "Both means that there's a line drawn somewhere, and while I can get really close to it, I can't cross over it."

She wasn't sure about a line, but she did know that there were certain things she wasn't willing to do with him.

"Are you going to give me any hints?" he asked.

"About the line?"

He nodded.

"No, I think you need to learn that all on your own."

They were flirting again, she thought with some surprise. They were having fun and talking and soon they would be kissing. "I didn't know it would be like this," she said without thinking.

"The truck, the great view or my incredible company?" he asked.

She laughed. "All of it."

"So the royal set is more reticent when they make out in their trucks."

She thought about her brief kisses in the past. They'd been chaste and uninspiring. "They don't generally make out in trucks, or in anything else."

"What? No foreplay. They just get right to it."

She could feel herself blushing. "No, it's not like that, either."

He leaned close and brushed a kiss against her mouth. "Am I talking too much?"

"No. I like the conversation. It relaxes me."

He moved to her cheek, then to her earlobe and nibbled. She shivered.

"Are you nervous?" he asked.

"Yes."

"Why?"

He pressed a damp kiss against the side of her neck. More shivers rippled through her as her breath caught and her heart rate increased. "Because I…"

He licked a sensitive spot right behind her ear, then slid his hands through her hair, tugging gently until she tilted her head back. Then he nipped the point of her chin before trailing kisses down the front of her throat.

"Go on," he murmured at the hollow of her throat. "I'm listening."

"You might be listening," she gasped, "but I'm having trouble speaking."

Shivers and heat and that wonderful tingling radiated from everywhere he touched. She held on to his upper arms, pressing her fingers into the thick muscles there. She'd read about passion before, had overheard conversations between women in airports or in boutiques, but she'd never experienced anything like it in her life. She'd even begun to wonder if there was something wrong with her. After all, she'd never felt that she was missing out on anything. She thought she might be one of those people who simply didn't have a strong physical connection or need.

But now, with Mitch holding her and kissing her, she knew that she'd been too quick in her assumption that the problem was with her. Obviously she'd just never been kissed the right way...or kissed the right man.

The latter thought terrified her, so she pushed it away. Experience, she thought dreamily as he circled the hollow of her throat with his tongue, was a wonderful thing. At least now she would have a benchmark by which to measure other men. Except she didn't want to think about being with other men. She only wanted to be with Mitch and have him keep touching her exactly as he was.

He pulled her closer. She started to move toward him, but their legs bumped.

"This isn't working," he grumbled, then placed his hands on her waist. "Am I allowed to touch the royal body or would that be a violation of your parameter?"

She tried to smile, to match his teasing mood. "I believe we might allow that to happen this one time."

"We?"

She sniffed. "The royal we."

"Ah. The rest of us are very grateful for your generosity. Now slide that long, gorgeous leg of yours across my lap and have a seat, young lady."

He shifted her until she was straddling him. As she did so, he slid lower in the seat so that when she lowered her weight, the heated place between her legs came down squarely on something hard and thick and very male.

His hands moved to her hips and he adjusted her slightly. "Perfect," he murmured, then pressed his mouth to hers.

Her mind raced in a thousand different directions, even as she instinctively responded to his kiss. She clung to his shoulders, more because she felt herself spinning out of control than because she needed to touch him, although she did need to feel his strength. Sensations from different parts of her body collected in her brain until there was too much information with too much happening at once.

Even as she moved her tongue against his and found herself drowning in his kiss, she couldn't ignore his strong fingers kneading her hips and holding her against him. Against his…his…

Alex shuddered, afraid to even think what it was.

He was aroused. Even as inexperienced as she was, she knew that much. He pressed close to her, a hard ridge that seemed so male and aggressive against her damp melting center. Then there was the intimacy of their position and the way he'd shifted her so easily, as if the female body and all the possibilities were familiar to him.

Why wouldn't they be? she asked herself. After all, he'd been married before. No doubt there had been other women, too. Girlfriends. Women on the rodeo circuit. What had he called them? Buckle bunnies?

She would have thought that she would find his experience intimidating, but instead she found herself grateful that one of them knew what they were doing. Based on the way he kissed her and held her, she had a feeling that Mitch had assumed she wasn't a virgin. A voice inside of her warned that if she told him the truth, he would stop what he was doing and get her back to the ranch as quickly as he could.

She didn't want that. She didn't want him to stop because she was enjoying everything he was doing. She wanted to know what happened between a man and a woman. Well, maybe not all of it—she didn't think she was ready to let go of her virginity—but she wanted to do at least a few things she'd only read about.

"I can't believe what you do to me," he murmured against her mouth. "You feel so good, taste so good."

She wanted to respond in kind, but she was two-parts embarrassed and one-part shy. She settled on breathing his name.

His hands moved up from her hips to her waist, then continued higher. She knew what he was going to do even before he touched her. Her breasts swelled in anticipation. She could feel her tight nipples straining against the inside of her silk bra. Her entire body tensed and she pulled back from his kiss so she could really think about what he was doing.

Slowly, more slowly, he drew his hands up her ribs. Closer and closer until she couldn't breathe, couldn't do anything but wait. Then strong hands closed over her breasts.

The sensation was more incredible than she'd imagined. He held her gently, almost with reverence. When he captured her lower lip in his teeth, she didn't even think about pulling back. He gently nibbled her sensitive skin, even as his forefinger and thumb closed over her nipple.

The combination of movements and the indescribable waves of pleasure that rushed through her made her unable to think or react. All she could do was feel—feel and silently beg him never to stop.

He read her mind. As he kissed her, then deepened the kiss, he continued to touch her breasts. He stroked them, encircled them, always coming back to tease her sensitive nipples. She grasped his face in her hands and plunged her tongue into his mouth. The passion inside of her grew until she felt it taking control. She wanted. She needed. And only Mitch had the magic necessary to make her whole.

When he removed his hands from her breasts, she whimpered.

"It's all right, darlin'," he soothed. "I'm not going anywhere."

She felt him unbuttoning the front of her shirt. Without meaning to, she found herself pulling the hem free of her jeans. Then his hands were on her bare ribs. He stroked her skin as he circled behind her and unfastened her bra.

"I want to see you," he said, his voice low and hoarse.

She looked at his face. In the semidarkness, his eyes were black and bottomless, but she saw the fire flickering there. She might not know much about men, but she knew that Mitch wanted her desperately. The knowledge, unexpected and delightful, gave her courage. She shrugged out of her shirt.

The night air was cool on her skin. As she pulled her arms out of her sleeves, her bra slipped down and she tossed that aside as well.

Mitch swore softly, then flashed her a smile. "I knew you'd be pretty, but I had no idea you'd be perfect."

Alex glanced down and saw how her pale breasts gleamed. Her throat tightened as she watched as well as felt his hands cup her curves, then stroke her skin. Without knowing why she did it, she found herself moving her hips back and forth, brushing her center against his hardness. Mitch groaned.

"Put your shirt back on," he said.

"What?"

He picked up the garment and held it out to her. "Just slip it on, but keep it open in front. I want to see you and touch you, but we *are* in the front seat of my truck. I don't want you flashing the world."

She'd forgotten that they were out in the open, where anyone might see them. "Thank you," she whispered, then pulled her shirt on over her arms and shoulders, leaving the fabric gaping in front.

He bent forward and kissed between her breasts. She wrapped her arms around his neck, burying her fingers in his thick brown hair. When his mouth closed over one nipple, she arched into him and had to bite back the scream forming low in her throat. Was it really supposed to be like this? Was making love so incredibly wonderful?

"Do you like that?" he asked.

"Oh, yes." She barely breathed the words. "Don't stop."

He chuckled against her skin. Warm puffs of air that made her rock her hips faster. She noticed a tension building inside of her. Low in her stomach, and in her legs. It was heavy and tight at the same time. Something was happening, but she didn't understand what.

"I'm not going to go all the way," he said quietly. "But I do want to touch you."

Alex couldn't figure out what he meant. He *was* touching her. She didn't want him to ever stop. She moved her hips slightly, trying to find a different position as she rubbed against him. One that would—

She felt his fingers at the waistband of her jeans and she froze. When he'd said touch her, had he meant *there?* They couldn't—she couldn't. Except she wanted him to. She wanted to feel…something, although she couldn't say what.

Then, before she could figure out how to tell him she was nervous and afraid and not too sure about all of this, he'd lowered the zipper and started tugging on her jeans.

"You want me to take them off?" she asked, hoping she didn't sound as shocked as she felt.

"That's the general idea."

"But I'll be naked."

He flashed her a grin. "You'll still have your shirt on." The smile faded. "I meant what I said, Alex. I won't go any further, but I do want to touch you. All of you."

She thought about how wonderful it had felt when he'd stroked and kissed her breasts. Was what he planned to do better than that? Was that possible? She found herself very interested in finding out.

So, in the middle of Arizona, in the front seat of a man's truck, Princess Alexandra of Wynborough pulled off her jeans and panties. Her parents would have died from the shock, she thought as she shivered in the cool night air. *She* might die from the shock.

Mitch's breath came out in a long hiss when she tossed her clothing aside and once again straddled him. "I can't tell you how much I want you," he breathed. "You're so beautiful and so sexy."

She'd never felt sexy before, not even once. She thought she was attractive, but no man had ever found himself swept away by her charms.

"Really?"

"Oh, yeah. There's a better-than-even chance that you're going to make me embarrass myself."

She wanted to ask how, but before she could, he put his hands on her thighs.

He was warm and sure as he touched her. The tension inside of her doubled then tripled as he slid up toward her most central place. Her breathing increased. She wanted to shriek and run away. She wanted to beg him to hurry. She settled on kissing him deeply.

As her tongue slipped into his mouth, she felt his thumbs sweep up her inner thighs. Her body tensed. Then a single finger slipped between the curls and stroked her. She'd thought she might feel invaded or violated, but instead it was exactly right. Mitch moved slowly, discovering her, just as she discovered what it felt like to have a man exploring her secret place. He moved back and forth, then side to side, touching, teasing, making her tense and shudder and squeak.

With his other hand he reached around and rubbed her fanny. The combination of attention made her hips pulse in little thrusting movements. When he slowly inserted a finger inside of her, she found herself sinking lower, wanting him deeper. He moved in and out in a rhythm that matched her own frantic movements. Then he pressed his thumb into the swollen folds of her flesh, searching, probing, touching until he found a single spot that made her gasp.

"Mitch," she breathed.

It was better than what he'd done with her breasts. It was better than anything she'd ever experienced before. She didn't know she could feel this much pleasure and live.

He brought his free hand up and cupped her right breast. As his tongue danced with hers, he worked magic on her nipple and between her legs. A long finger moved in and out. His thumb circled that one incredible spot she hadn't even known existed.

She clutched at him, at his head, his shoulders. She strained toward him, pulsing and pushing into his touch, urging him deeper and faster. The tension increased until she thought she was going to explode or die or find paradise. She parted her legs more, sank into him, then found herself shaking uncontrollably. Her body was no longer hers to command. It was Mitch, only Mitch, who shaped her destiny.

He shifted his hands beneath her, then she felt the thick pressure of two fingers thrusting inside of her. It was too intense, too wonderful. She held on to him and waited for the explosion.

It began with a trembling in her thighs and her belly, then rocketed out until even her skin quivered. Bursts of pleasure filled her, spilling out, making her tense and release and push and gasp, until she was spent and could only sag against him.

Alex felt as if she'd almost lost consciousness. Nothing in her previous life had prepared her for this moment. She slowly became aware of her surroundings to find Mitch holding her tenderly as he rained soft kisses all over her face.

"Thank you," he whispered against her mouth.

"I think that's supposed to be my line," she murmured.

"I loved doing that to you."

She pressed her lips together to keep from telling him to feel free to indulge whenever he might like. She hadn't known that her body was capable of such incredible sensations. Looked as though she had a passionate nature, after all.

She gave a brief thought to her nakedness, but before she could get embarrassed, Mitch was helping her slip on her panties, then her jeans. He kissed her breasts and now-sensitive nipples, before sliding on her bra, then her shirt. In less than five minutes she was dressed and curled up next to him on the bench seat of his truck.

"Thank you for everything," she said softly.

"You're welcome. I've had a really good time tonight. But I should probably get you home before your folks start to worry."

It took her a minute to remember the game they'd started earlier, about being two teenagers parked out here for a make-out session.

"I wish I'd known you then," she said. "Back when we were young."

"We're hardly old now."

"I know, but it's different."

He started the truck engine and headed back for the main road. They drove in silence for several minutes, then he took her hand, brought it to his mouth and kissed her fingers. "I wish that, too."

Mitch stood naked in front of his bedroom window and watched the sun come up over the eastern mountains. The room was cold, nearly cold enough to distract him from the discomfort of his erection. He'd been hard since he'd first kissed Alex the previous night, and he'd stayed that way all through his restless night.

Sleep had been impossible. Some of it was the physical manifestation of his desire for her, but some of it was the different thoughts flashing through his brain. Thoughts that boiled down to one main thrust—he was getting in way over his head.

He'd recited the facts a thousand times. She was royalty. She might even become queen of her country. Someone like her wasn't going to be interested in someone like him, and even if she was, their lives had nothing in common. There was no way in hell she was going to give it all up to live on a ranch, taking care of horses and cattle while raising three or four kids. He knew enough about himself to know that he would never be happy in her world even if she invited him for a test drive. So what was he thinking?

Last night had been a mistake, he thought to himself. He never should have taken her to Submarine Point. He certainly never should have kissed her or touched her or… His body flexed in reaction to his thoughts. To the memories of the taste of her and the feel of her. He recalled every second of their time together, especially the way she'd responded so exquisitely to his touch. When she'd climaxed, he'd watched the pleasure tighten the muscles of her face, even as he'd felt the rippling contractions around his fingers buried deep inside of her. He couldn't help wondering how it would have felt if he'd buried himself inside of her instead.

"Don't go there," he said aloud. It was dangerous territory. Nothing was going to happen between him and Alex. He couldn't let himself fall for her. If he ever married again, he needed it to be for sensible reasons to a woman who understood his life-style and wanted the same things he did. He'd learned a lot from his first marriage, and one of the most important lessons was that love wasn't always enough to make something last.

Chapter Eleven

Alex tried to pay attention to what her mother was saying, but she found herself drifting back in time to all that had happened with Mitch the previous night. She hadn't been able to think about anything else. Not on the drive home, not while she lay in bed, unable to sleep, not that morning while she'd been showering and dressing.

Everything was different, although she couldn't exactly say how. Maybe it was her heightened awareness of the world around her, as if she'd suddenly realized all the vivid colors and sounds that filled her day. Maybe it was her sense of her own body, of the texture of her skin and hair, of the incredibly intricate marvel of engineering that was the human body.

And when she wasn't stumbling around like an alien discovering a new planet, she was reliving every moment of their time together, from their conversation in the diner to the way he'd touched her when they'd been in his truck. She still couldn't believe her body was capable of those amazing sensations. What had she been missing all her life?

Except… Alex drew in a deep breath. Except her instinct told her that what had happened between Mitch and her had been special. Not that another man wouldn't make her enjoy intimacy, but with Mitch there had been an extra jolt of chemistry. She had a feeling that being with someone else wasn't going to be as wonderful, nor would she feel as safe and comfortable after the fact. Which was all too confusing.

If she was right, then what did that mean? She searched her heart to find out if she had any regrets about what they'd done, and she found she didn't. She trusted Mitch. He wouldn't go running off to share details with a tabloid. He wouldn't use their intimacy against her, or try to make her feel obligated or cheap. He was a good man.

"If you're trying to pretend you're listening, you're not doing a very good job."

Her mother's voice jolted her out of her reverie. "Sorry," Alex said. "I was—"

"Woolgathering. Yes, I could tell. Do you want to tell me what's going on?"

"Nothing really. I have a lot of things to do today."

"You're not a very good liar, Alexandra. Does this have anything to do with the reason you're not with your sisters in Aspen?"

Alex opened her mouth, but no words emerged.

Had her parents guessed what was going on? "Not at all."

"I see." Her mother's voice was clipped. "You're not staying at a resort, are you? I was surprised when you first said you were relaxing at a spa. Elizabeth might do that, or even Serena, but never you. You're not the spa type."

"I'm..." She straightened in her chair, as if her mother could see through the telephone lines, not to mention across the thousands of miles, and comment on her posture. "I'm staying at a working ranch. You're right, I would be bored silly at a spa, but I did want to get away. The owners have let me set up an office here. I work in the morning, then ride in the afternoon. I'm having a wonderful time."

She bit her lower lip and wondered if her mother was going to believe this cleaned-up version of the truth. The only thing she was leaving out was the ongoing search for James...and her relationship with Mitch.

"It's more than that," her mother said, then sighed. "What is it, my dear? I can hear something in your voice. Something..." The older woman gave a short laugh. "If I didn't know better, I would say there was a man involved."

Alex didn't want to know how her mother had guessed. Maybe it was some secret learned while raising her four daughters. At least she hadn't guessed about the investigation.

She was about to deny the presence of any significant man when she realized she desperately wanted to talk about Mitch to someone who would understand. "It's not what you think," she began slowly.

"I don't know what *to* think," her mother admitted. "If you're attracted to someone, I must confess to being relieved. I was never happy about your decision not to get emotionally involved with someone inappropriate."

"You wanted me to fall in love with someone I shouldn't?" Alex asked, stunned.

"Not at all. My complaint was with your determination to keep your heart so completely closed off until a political match could be made. You are impossibly practical, Alexandra. Just once I would like you to be impulsive, to act with your heart, rather than your head."

"Serena does that enough for all of us," Alex said.

"Perhaps, and at times she's found her way into trouble, but I would guess her happiness is guaranteed. She will always do what is right for her, rather than what is correct for the kingdom."

"That's irresponsible."

"Perhaps, but who will have the better life?" Her mother paused. "I want you to be happy, too, my dear. Life is more than duty. So if you've finally noticed an inappropriate but handsome, charming man, I'm pleased. Tell me about him."

Alex was still dealing with all that her mother had said. "I have duties."

"Yes, I know. But sometimes it's important to remember the duties to one's self. Personal happiness is allowed. Everything doesn't have to be for the greater good. Now, what about this mystery man?"

Alex leaned back in her chair and smiled. "His name is Mitch. He is handsome and charming, but those are the least of his qualities. He's strong and sure of himself, yet very gentle. He keeps forgetting that I'm a princess, Mother. He treats me like a normal woman."

"Ah, that *would* be hard to resist."

"It is. And he's honest and stubborn and can be difficult."

"But you like that about him."

Alex laughed. "I do," she admitted. "I like that he doesn't back down from me. I don't frighten him with either my title or my strength of character. But..." Her voice trailed off. She drew in a breath. "But he's tied to the land. He's a rancher and all he wants is here."

"What do you want?"

"I don't know. I want to be happy. I want to fulfill my responsibilities. I want to do the right thing." She squeezed her eyes shut. "What if I become queen? Mitch would never be comfortable in the role of consort. He would never want to leave his ranch, and even if he did, even if he was willing to try, it would destroy him. All that I admire about him would be crushed. Then where would we be?"

"It's quite a problem. What does Mitch say about it?"

"You mean have I talked to him about this?"

"Yes."

"Of course not. I wouldn't discuss this with him."

"So you've met a man whom you admire greatly.

You're in fact falling in love with him, but you refuse to discuss the future with him.''

Alex opened her mouth, then closed it. "I don't love him.''

"Of course you don't. It would never work. How smart you are to figure this out early. I assume you'll be leaving today?''

"Leaving?''

"Yes. Why waste your time being around a man like him? If he won't compromise and give up his world for you, why bother with him?''

"It's not like that. I'm not saying that he wouldn't give up everything, I'm saying I don't want him to.''

"But you don't love him.''

"No.'' She couldn't. Love Mitch? It wasn't possible. Things could never work out between them. They were too different. Love. She thought about how he'd held her the previous night, and the way he'd laughed with her in the diner. She thought about his strong, gentle hands and the way he made her feel as if she belonged in his arms. Was that love?

"No,'' she said firmly. "We're friends. Nothing more.''

"Alexandra, you are a most stubborn woman. I suppose I should be grateful you've learned there's more to life than simply doing your duty. So take your newfound knowledge and start enjoying yourself. Stop faxing the palace four and five times a day. Stop calling. We're fine here. We have a staff that functions surprisingly well despite your absence. Why don't you take a trip to Disneyland or go see a play in New York? Or better yet, have a wild, passionate affair with your young man.''

''Mother!''

The queen laughed. ''Don't for a moment think that your generation invented sex. It's actually been around for quite some time.''

''I know that. I just can't believe you would encourage reckless behavior in one of your daughters.''

''I wouldn't, Alexandra. I trust you to temper a little bit of wildness with good sense. If you trust this Mitch, then I believe he is trustworthy. So have fun for once. Worry about the rest of it when you're back in Wynborough.'' She paused, then spoke to someone at the other end of the phone. ''I must go. I love you.''

''I love you, too.''

Alex hung up the phone and stared at the receiver. Her mother wanted her to have an affair? Or at the very least, enjoy herself with Mitch. Was that possible? Was it even allowed?

Alex petted the smooth, soft nose of the skittish bay mare. ''There's a pretty girl. Aren't you lovely? Don't you like your new home?''

Alex hadn't tried riding the new mare yet, but she was making progress. Princess—Alex still smiled every time she thought of the bay's name—trusted her enough to take bits of apple or carrot from her hand. The horse even let her stroke her nose and rub her ears. But Alex sensed that there would be trouble if the animal was ridden too early.

''I had the most interesting conversation with my

mother this morning,'' Alex said as she collected brushes and combs and stepped inside the stall to groom the mare. "Parents can be very unusual. Just when I think I have my mother completely figured out, she does something to shock me. Are you like that with your babies?''

The mare's only response was to toss her head.

"I thought so.'' Alex brushed the mare's coat with long, slow, steady strokes. She was trying to get the animal used to her presence, her voice and her touch. "When we're done in here, I'm going to take you out and exercise you on a lead.''

She reached up and brushed Princess's neck. "She told me it's time for me to put aside my responsibilities and have a little fun. The thing is, I'm not sure I remember how. I've been so responsible for so long. What if that's all I know?''

Princess looked at her as if urging her to continue with her story.

"I'm the oldest of four daughters,'' Alex said. "I was always expected to be the most mature, to do the right thing and set an example for my sisters. Even when I wanted to play with them, or with my friends, I often had duties and responsibilities. It wasn't that easy for me to be like other children. If my sisters didn't want to go to a function, they often were allowed to refuse. But I had to be there. As I grew older, there were more functions and more responsibilities. Not that I minded. I always felt it was my place to serve.''

She walked around the front of the horse and began brushing the other side. "Somehow I've come to believe I have to earn my place in the world. I know that probably sounds silly, but it's true. Even with all the family wealth and privilege, I worry about not being enough, or doing enough. It was as if I'd been given so much that I had to prove I was worthy of keeping it. So many times I've admired my sisters and wished I could be more like them. Katherine is so calm and relaxed. Nothing ruffles her. She never has any self-doubts. Elizabeth has a zest for life that inspires me, even as I envy her. And Serena, well, she can be a force of nature. She is impulsive and while she frustrates me, in my heart I wish I could be more like her.''

She pressed her hands against the mare's side. ''I've always been so dependable and boring. I've never dared to do what I wanted with my life.''

''What do you want?''

She jumped at the sound of the male voice, then spun on her heel. Mitch leaned against the half door of the stall. He rested his elbows on the flat top and turned his hat in his outstretched hands.

''What do you want, Alex?''

His gaze was steady and direct. She supposed she should be embarrassed. After all, this was the first time they'd run into each other since parting the previous night. But she wasn't nervous or ashamed or anything but pleased to see him.

''I don't know,'' she admitted. ''I'm torn between duty and fun.''

''Is this fun?'' he asked, motioning to the ranch.

''Yes, as are you.''

''Good. So why can't you have both?''

"It's not always that easy." She stroked the mare's neck. "I spoke with my mother this morning. To quote American television, she told me to get a life."

"Sounds like good advice."

She wondered what he would say if she told him that her mother had also told her to have an affair with him.

"I suppose it is. But I don't know that I can have a life without duty."

"You can. You're just not sure you know how."

"You're right." She squeezed the brush in her hand. "I think about James, about us finding him. What I don't allow myself to think about very much is what will happen if we don't find him. What will my future be?"

"Only you can answer that." Mitch's brown eyes darkened with compassion and something that might have been concern. "Although if you became queen, it would certainly change things."

Was he talking about her...or them?

"How long are you going to wait to have your future decided by outside forces?" he asked. "When do you get a vote?"

"I'm not sure that I do."

"But it's your life."

She nodded. "This is where I start to get confused. At what point does my personal responsibility to myself end and my duty to my country begin?"

"Can't you have both? Personal happiness and duty?"

"Perhaps."

But not with him, she thought, studying his handsome face. He would never be happy away from the ranch, and knowing that, she would never ask him to leave.

Her train of thought should have terrified her. It implied a deep affection that she wasn't sure she felt. At least, she didn't think she was sure. If she'd never really been involved with a man before, how was she supposed to know what was real and what wasn't?

Mitch turned his hat around in his hands. "Are you okay?"

"I'm fine."

He smiled. "No, Alex. I'm asking if you're all right about last night."

"Oh." Heat instantly flared in her cheeks. She swallowed and forced herself to meet his gaze, even though all she wanted to do was bury her face in the mare's sleek neck. "Yes, I, uh, am perfectly fine with all that happened."

"Good."

His gaze slid away from hers, and she realized he was nervous, too. That made her feel a little better.

"You know, I've done that sort of thing before," he said. "Sex, I mean."

"So I assumed."

"Yeah, well, the point is, I know the difference between sex and something more."

What could be more? she wondered. "You're talking about the act versus..."

"Feelings. Connection." He cleared his throat. The hat in his hands spun faster. "I don't have all the answers."

She hadn't realized there had been questions. Alex

didn't know whether to laugh or sit down and cry her eyes out. For as long as she lived, she knew she would remember this moment: the scent of the straw and horses; Mitch's nervous fingers betraying his tension; the way his dark hair fell over his forehead; and her own desire to go to him and be held.

"I doubt anyone has *all* the answers," she said.

"Agreed." He looked at her. "I don't know what it was, but I know it was more. Which makes the whole thing scary, but in a good way." He stopped spinning his hat. "I want you, but becoming lovers is going to complicate things a whole lot more than either of us realizes. Or maybe you know because you've done this sort of thing before."

He wanted her? In his bed? The thought was thrilling. Impossible, but thrilling.

Alex wondered if she should take this opportunity to clear up his misconception about her experience level. Then she decided that if Mitch knew she was a virgin, he would take off running for the very picturesque mountains behind the ranch, and she would never see him again.

"It *would* change things," she agreed.

"That's what I thought. So I figured the best thing would be for us to just back off. For a while at least. Until we figure out what we want."

Was he talking about life in general or them in particular? What did he want? What was he saying? That they might have a chance at a regular relationship? Did he care about her? She knew that he liked her, but was he talking about being more than friends?

Too many questions and absolutely no answers.

"I'll see you at dinner," Mitch said, and turned to leave.

Princess Alexandra, who had been told she was imperious and bossy, couldn't find the courage to stop him so she could ask him what he meant.

"So much for the power of royalty," she murmured to the mare when they were alone. "Apparently in the whole man-woman game, having a tiara doesn't matter for spit."

Chapter Twelve

"I'm going to be cleaning pie dough off the ceiling for weeks," Betty complained good-naturedly.

Alex looked at the flour covering the countertop around her, not to mention the light dusting that climbed nearly to her elbows as she rolled out her piecrust. She grinned. "I warned you that I'd never made a pie before. My cooking classes never covered them." She paused, trying to remember all her instructors had discussed. "I'm great at tortes and cakes and can make you a dozen perfect roses in marzipan, but pies are a mystery. Especially pumpkin."

Betty arched her eyebrows and looked suitably shocked. "It's a tradition."

"I know. But I must remind you that I've never really celebrated Thanksgiving. It's strictly an American holiday."

"I hadn't thought of that," Betty admitted. She stood at the stove, stirring a sugar-and-evaporated-milk mixture that was the basis of what Mitch had promised was killer fudge. "So you've never had a real Thanksgiving dinner?"

"I vaguely remember my mother insisting on turkey dinner a few times when I was growing up, but somehow the celebration got lost." Alex shrugged. "There are so many events going on at any one time. The palace sponsors many of the arts. Then there are the visiting dignitaries, not to mention our own national holidays."

Betty pulled the heavy pot off the burner and poured in a bowl of chocolate chips. "When you're all gussied up in one of your suits, talking on the phone or getting something messengered to you, it's easy to think of you as a princess. But now, you're just like a regular person."

Alex carefully folded the crust in quarters, then lifted it to the pie pan and unfolded it. She glanced at Betty. "That must mean I have pie dough in my hair."

"Nope, but you have flour on your face."

Alex started to wipe it away, then realized her hands were too dirty to be of any help. "If someone sneaks up and takes a photo, I'll simply claim to be setting a new style."

"You do that," Betty said. "I'm sure they'll believe you."

Alex chuckled as she crimped the edge of the pie-crust in place. When she'd finished, Betty nodded to the remaining dough. "Now do it all again. You're making three pies all together."

"But what if they're terrible?"

"We're using my secret recipe, so they're going to be terrific. Don't you worry about how they'll taste."

"I hope you're right," Alex said doubtfully.

"Trust me. We'll be turning you into a pastry chef in no time." Betty stirred a cup of nuts into the rapidly thickening fudge. "So how's the search for your long-lost brother coming?"

"I'm not sure," Alex admitted. "I've been back to The Sunshine Home twice, and every time I'm there, the task of going through the records gets more and more daunting. Mitch helped me sort the boxes by year and subject, but then when I started searching through them I realized that what the label said and what was in the boxes were two very different things. Apparently people have searched for records before, but they didn't file things back where they belonged. I think I'm going to have to talk to my sisters and have one or two of them come here and help me."

"Sounds like a plan," Betty said. She glanced over and studied the way Alex rolled out the dough. "Just exactly like you're doing. Smooth and even."

Alex flashed her a grateful smile. "You're being very patient."

"I'm enjoying your company."

"I'm having fun, too," she said. If truth were told, she liked almost everything about her stay. Most especially Mitch. He was an unexpectedly wonderful bonus. If she was honest with herself, she didn't mind the time she'd had to spend here, nor did she mind that her sisters were too busy with public appearances to join her anytime soon. She wasn't sure she wanted either Elizabeth or Serena getting a look at her handsome cowboy host.

She finished with the second piecrust and started on the third. "My sister Katherine is busy tracking a lead right now, but I'm sure that Serena and Elizabeth will come to Hope eventually. We have to coordinate our schedules. Right now they're busy with personal appearances."

"Do you have any of those planned?"

"I have one on Saturday in Los Angeles. It's a large fund-raiser for a local cancer center. But other than that, I'm free until after the first of the year."

"Well, whenever your sisters arrive, they'll be welcome here."

"That would be too many of us," Alex said. "I think they'll be better off at a hotel."

Betty gave her a quick, knowing look but didn't say anything, except to direct her to pour the prepared pumpkin filling into the piecrusts. "Then we bake," the older woman said, "and tomorrow we'll taste them."

"Couldn't we taste one tonight and make sure that they're all right?"

"Have a little faith."

"Oh, I have plenty of faith," Alex murmured as she placed the three pies into the oven. "I'm just not so sure about my crust-making abilities."

"Just promise," Alex insisted several hours later as she and Mitch relaxed in the living room after dinner.

He made an X over his heart. "I promise I won't laugh at you tomorrow if your pumpkin pies are gross."

She reached behind her and grabbed one of the small, decorative cushions in the corner of the couch and threatened him with it. "I did *not* say they would be gross. I said I was the tiniest bit concerned about how they might taste and I wanted you to promise to be gentle."

His brown eyes darkened with an emotion that had nothing to do with her pies. "I will always be gentle with you, Alex."

How did he do that? she wondered as her thighs began to tremble and her heart thundered wildly against her breastbone. With just a sultry tone and a few casual words he reduced her to a quivering mass. She felt like a heroine from a daytime drama. One of those wild women who do anything for passion. Which didn't make sense. She was Princess Alexandra of Wynborough. She was neither passionate nor wild. So why was she so different when she was with Mitch?

"What are you thinking?" he asked. "You have the oddest expression on your face."

She shook her head. "Nothing really."

"Liar."

"All right. How about if I say that it's personal?"

"That I'll accept." He took a sip of his brandy, then grinned. "So, what were you thinking?"

This time she actually smacked him with the small,

fluffy cushion. He had the nerve to laugh at her. "Yeah, like that's going to hurt."

"You could at least pretend to be intimidated," she grumbled. "Need I remind you that I do have the power to behead you."

"Cheap talk. I'm starting to think you're not even a real princess."

She sat angled toward him, their knees bumping. A couple of floor lamps provided subdued lighting, as did the crackling fire. As she inhaled the sweet scent of wood smoke, Alex promised herself that no matter what happened, she would always remember this night. The way Mitch sat so close to her, the sensual, unspoken but very real promise between them. She wanted to hold all her memories from the ranch in a special place in her brain so she wouldn't lose a single detail. For reasons she didn't quite understand, she sensed that they were going to be a very important part of her life and not anything she would want to forget.

His gaze settled on her face. "But you are a real princess, aren't you. No matter that I wish you weren't."

His comment surprised her. "Why would you wish that?"

His only answer was a shrug.

Alex wasn't sure what to make of that. Her royal status shouldn't matter to him, unless he was talking about her invasion of his house. If she hadn't been royalty, there would have been no reason for her to have stayed this long. Except she didn't think that was what he meant.

"I'm glad you're going to be here for Thanksgiving," he said. "My folks wanted me to come up to Washington and stay with them, but I'd already decided I couldn't get away. You're going to save me from a very solitary dinner."

"I'm glad. I would hate to think that I was intruding on a carefully planned event."

"Not likely. Betty makes most of the meal beforehand. Last year John was around, but this year I was going to be all on my own."

Alex frowned. "I hadn't thought of this before, but I just realized that your brother is going to miss a very important family holiday. Would he really stay away and not even call you or your parents?"

Mitch shrugged. "He might. John has his own demons to deal with. I gave up judging him a long time ago."

There was something in Mitch's tone, a whisper of discontent, or was it anger? "Don't the two of you get along?"

Mitch was silent for a long time. He shifted so his head rested against the back of the sofa and his long legs stretched out in front of him. The movement meant they weren't touching anymore, and Alex tried hard not to feel abandoned. She could see that Mitch had lost himself in the past.

"We get along fine…now," he said slowly. "Since our late teens, we've been pretty close. But there were a lot of years I hated the sight of him."

She couldn't imagine hating one of her sisters. "Why?"

"Because I was afraid." He rested his hands on his

flat belly and drew in a deep breath. "I was four when my parents adopted John. They had explained to me that they wanted to give me a brother or sister but that they couldn't. I found out later that my mom had had some troubles during delivery and the doctors recommended she not have another baby. So they decided to adopt another child."

"Why would that frighten you?"

"I thought they were replacing me. I thought *they* thought I wasn't good enough, that they'd adopted John because they didn't think I would be able to handle the responsibility of the ranch. He was there as backup in case I screwed up."

"Did you ever discuss this with them?"

He shook his head. "Eventually I figured out that they'd really wanted another child, and that they thought a boy would be more fun for me. I let all the ambivalence go."

"Are you sure?" Alex asked before she could stop herself. Then she pressed her fingertips to her mouth. "Sorry, that just slipped out. You don't have to answer that question."

"I know, but it's a good point. Sometimes I still work the thought over in my mind and wonder if I'm good enough. But not very often and never for long. I do a good job here, and I know my parents are proud of me."

More important, he was proud of himself. But this time Alex managed to hold the words back.

"I worry about John," Mitch admitted. "No matter how my folks tried to make him feel like one of the family, he's never completely fit in. Even as a kid he seemed to be searching for something else.''

''Is that why he disappears?''

''I guess. Something out there keeps calling to him, and he keeps leaving to find it.''

Was John her long-lost brother, searching for his true identity, or was he just a man with a case of wanderlust? She didn't have the answer, and she wasn't even sure she wanted one. As much as she needed her future settled, Alex wasn't in any hurry to leave the ranch...and Mitch.

''We are so much alike,'' she mused. ''You and I,'' she added when he glanced at her and raised his eyebrows.

''What are you talking about? Little lady, we couldn't be more different.''

''You're wrong,'' she told him. ''Of course we're different in that respect. You're mostly wrong and I'm mostly right.''

The low growl in his throat warned her of the attack just microseconds before he launched himself at her. She shrieked and tried to scramble off the sofa, but he already had her pinned. His long, strong body held her firmly in place while his fingers searched out and found ticklish spots on her ribs.

''Stop,'' she gasped, trying to push him away. She laughed and yelped and squirmed, but nothing helped.

''You're just wasting energy, darlin'. I was on the rodeo circuit. If I can wrestle a two-thousand-pound steer to the ground, one skinny, redheaded princess isn't going to be much of a problem.''

She pushed at him, but it was like shoving against

the side of a mountain. He didn't budge. "Violence is the refuge of the incompetent," she said.

"Uh-huh. That's pretty high-and-mighty coming from someone so completely out of control of the situation." He tickled her ribs again.

"No!" She wiggled and squirmed, but it was no use. All she could do was try to capture his hands in hers and hold them. Unfortunately, he pulled free of her easily.

"Dammit, Mitch, let me go."

He raised his eyebrows in mock astonishment. "Was that profanity I heard falling from those royal lips?"

"Yes, and you're going to hear more." She glared at him. "And I'm not skinny."

"Did I say skinny?"

Her bangs were in her eyes. She pushed them out of the way. "You did."

"I apologize. You're slender, but in the most delightful way. All your curves are exactly as they should be."

"You would be the one to know," she grumbled.

His smile turned wolfish. "I would be, wouldn't I?"

They looked at each other. When he wasn't tickling her, she found that she liked being pinned by him. His legs tangled with hers and his mouth was so close, it wouldn't be difficult at all to kiss him. The thought made her shiver and sort of melt inside.

Was it her imagination or was he thinking the same thing? His eyes seemed so dilated, they were nearly black. Had his breathing increased?

''Tell me how we're alike,'' he said.

''What?''

''You told me that we were very much alike. I want to know how we're the same.''

Is that what he'd been thinking? While she'd been lost in the moment of their closeness, he'd been remembering a snippet of conversation? Obviously she would never understand men.

She started to straighten, but he didn't move. ''Aren't you going to let me up?''

''No.''

''Oh.'' She blinked. ''All right.'' She took a couple of seconds to try to remember what she'd been thinking when she made the comment about them being similar in nature.

''We're both the oldest,'' she said. ''We have a strong sense of tradition and of doing the right thing. We believe in the past, but we also look to the future.''

''I see. If you put it that way, I guess you're right. I just never saw myself as anything like royalty.''

He chuckled, but suddenly Alex didn't find his comment funny.

''Why do you keep doing that?'' she asked. ''Why do you keep talking about me being a princess?''

''Because you are.''

''I know that. But the way you say it, it's almost as if you're reminding yourself.''

His humor faded. ''Maybe I am.''

''Why? Am I so very different? Can't you treat me like any other woman in your life?''

''But you're not like them.''

. He wasn't making any sense. "What am I doing wrong?" she demanded. "Tell me how I'm different."

"You just are."

"That's not an answer."

"It's the best I can do."

"So you'll never treat me like everyone else."

His mouth pulled into a straight line. "What do you want to know, Alex? What's the point here?"

"I don't know. I just wish—" She drew in a deep breath. "I wish you didn't think of me as different. I wish you wouldn't always worry about the whole princess issue."

"I don't."

"Of course you do. Everything is different because of who I am and how you think you should treat me."

"It's not as different as you think."

She knew she was acting like an eight-year-old, but she couldn't seem to help herself. "So if I wasn't a princess, everything about our relationship would be the same?"

He hesitated long enough for her to know that she'd hit on some truth.

"What?" she asked. "What would be different?"

He started to pull away. She grabbed on to his arms. "Mitch, tell me."

"You think you're so damn smart, don't you?" He glared at her. "All right, princess, try this one on for size. If you weren't my guest and my responsibility, not to mention royalty, I would toss you over my shoulder, carry you down the hall to my bedroom and make love with you until this time next week."

Chapter Thirteen

He was certainly direct, Alex thought in numb disbelief as she tried to figure out if Mitch had really said he wanted to make love with her or if she'd imagined it. She prayed it was the former, rather than the latter, because the thought of him wanting her that much made her want to throw herself at him and beg him to show her exactly what happened between a man and a woman.

"At least you didn't hit me," he said, then cast her a sideways glance. "I probably shouldn't have said that, but you were pushing me for an answer, and that's the only one I could think of."

Her excitement faded as quickly as it had flared. "It was just a line?" she asked, trying hard to keep the disappointment from her voice.

He sat up straight. ''Of course not. What kind of jerk do you think I am?''

''I don't think you're a jerk at all. I just wasn't sure what you meant.'' She had the uncomfortable feeling that their conversation had just taken a turn for the worse.

''I meant—'' he shook his head ''—hell, I don't know what I meant. The truth is you tie me up in knots. You have from the first moment you sashayed onto this ranch, looking like a million bucks in your city clothes and that pitiful excuse for a car.''

She bristled. The Jaguar had been a reckless purchase—one of the few she'd ever allowed herself in her life. ''What's wrong with my car?''

''Nothing. It's beautiful and impractical and has no business being here.'' He reached out and stroked her cheek. ''Just like you, princess. Just like you.''

''Oh, Mitch.'' She felt herself leaning toward him. ''Is this crazy?''

''Only if you want me as much as I want you.''

Wanting. What did it feel like exactly? Alex wasn't sure she knew. She'd never talked about the sensation with anyone before, mostly because it had never been an issue in her life. She'd been so sure she would be married by now and that she would experience whatever passion was to be in her life as a married woman. But she hadn't married, and so far her parents showed no signs of finding her a husband. Were they waiting for her?

The thought that she might have some control over her own destiny was so startling that she very nearly forgot about the tender touch of Mitch's fingers against her cheek. Except the tingling reminded her. As did the ache in her breasts and the strong pulsing low in her stomach. Was this passion? The need to be very close to a specific man. The desire for him to hold her close and touch all of her, to teach her about lovemaking and let her explore him? Because if that was wanting, then she wanted Mitch very much. She wanted him more than she'd ever wanted anything in her life.

"It's crazy," she whispered, telling herself that she was nearly thirty and she'd been a virgin plenty long enough.

He cupped her face. She saw him swallow and felt the fire leap from him. It circled her body, then ignited more flames within her body. She trembled and felt an answering shudder from him.

"I want you so bad, I can't figure out if I'm in heaven or hell," he told her. "But you're not an ordinary woman."

When she would have spoken, he touched a finger to her mouth. "I'm not just talking about the whole princess thing," he said. "You're very special. We haven't gone into details about our past love lives, but I suspect you've been real particular about who you've let in your bed." His brown eyes darkened. "I respect that, Alex. I respect you."

The realization that they might actually do this… this…act together sent more heat flooding her. It also unleashed an entire herd of nerves. She couldn't, could she? What if he figured out she was a virgin? Here Mitch was telling her that he would respect her in the morning, but that was based on his assumption that she'd been with other men. Or at least one other man. Thank goodness he didn't consider her wildly experienced. Oh, why hadn't she asked her mother more questions about sex? Make that any questions. Alex suddenly remembered she didn't know much more than she'd read or that she and her sisters had speculated about years before when they'd all been innocent teenagers. For all she knew each of her sisters kept a stable of lovers and she was the only ignorant one in the bunch.

"You're awfully quiet," he said. "Having a change of heart?"

He kept his tone light, but she read the tension in his body. She knew Mitch well enough to believe that if she said she didn't want to go through with this, he would understand completely. He would never pressure her or say anything unkind. But what about after? What if he figured out about her lack of experience? Would he think less of her?

"I'm just thinking," she told him. "I'm not having second thoughts, at least not in the way you're thinking. I'm less worried about your respect than our friendship. Will we still be friends in the morning?"

He laughed. "Darlin', if it's as good as I think it's going to be between us, I might want to be your lapdog more than your friend, but yes, we'll still be fine."

"Prove it," she said.

"What? How?"

She thought quickly. Whatever happened between them tonight, she didn't want to lose Mitch. He treated her like a regular person and liked her for her.

In her world, that was a special gift she intended to keep as long as possible.

"Come with me on Saturday."

His gaze narrowed. "Where are you going?"

"Los Angeles. I have to attend a charity fund-raiser for a cancer hospital." She started speaking more quickly. "I'm only asking you to go with me. You wouldn't have to say anything or even talk to anyone if you didn't want to."

He dropped his hands to his lap. "Let me see if I have this straight. You want me to come with you to some fancy-pants shindig this Saturday. You want me to face reporters and those rich city folk, not to mention a plane ride, all so that you'll know that whatever happens between us tonight, we're still friends?"

She lowered her gaze. When he said it like that, she didn't know how to respond. "I see your point," she murmured. "I didn't mean to make such a big deal about it. I just…" She'd just wanted the fantasy, she realized. She'd wanted her handsome lover at her side on Saturday. She'd wanted to show him off and know that he was nearby. Selfishly she'd wanted someone to lean on. She who had never wanted to lean on anyone before.

She didn't just like and trust Mitch, Alex thought. She needed him. Somehow he'd become important to her, more important than she'd known until that very moment.

"Alex? Look at me."

Slowly she raised her head until she stared at his face. He leaned forward and kissed her. "Yes, I'll come to the fund-raiser."

She wasn't sure which had caught her attention more, his announcement or the hard, hot pressure of his mouth against hers. "You will?"

"Of course. I want to be with you, to spend time with you. If promising you this relaxes you, then I'm happy to do it. I'll do it even if you don't want to make love, although I'll probably be more grumpy." He stood up and pulled her to her feet. "I'll smile for the reporters, I'll make polite conversation with the society crowd, I'll even dance."

He drew her close and took her in his arms, then demonstrated with a couple of steps. "Are you impressed?"

Her heart thundered inside her chest, and she thought her knees were going to fail her. "More than you know."

"I care about you," he said, wrapping his arms around her waist. "You're my favorite princess in the whole world."

She laughed. "I'm the only princess you know."

He winked. "That will be our little secret." He stepped back and held out his hand. "Join me?"

He was nothing that she'd expected in her life, but then the best things were often those found when people weren't looking. She'd thought her first experience with a man would be different, as well. But as she stepped toward him and placed her fingers on his palm, she knew that no other moment would ever feel so incredibly right.

"I'm scared," she said as he led her down the hall.

"You're scared? If I mess up, you can have me beheaded. Talk about performance pressure."

Despite her attempts to convince him that she was nervous, he had her laughing by the time they walked into his bedroom. Then, as she took in the large four-poster bed and the stone fireplace in the corner, she froze.

Mitch drew her to him instantly. "Don't start thinking about all those doubts and questions. It all comes down to two things—do you want to do this and do you trust me?"

She tried to speak, but her throat was too tight. Yet she needed him to know the truth. So instead of words, she tried actions. Her wool shirtwaist dress fastened in the front. She reached up and unfastened the top button of her dress.

Mitch swallowed hard and told himself he had to be dreaming. No way was he really standing in his bedroom with a beautiful, sassy, funny woman who was going out of her way to tell him that she wanted him. This wasn't happening. He'd had a good life, but he'd never had this kind of luck.

"Alex," he breathed, and stilled her fingers with his. He searched her face, first with his gaze, then with his fingers, gently tracing her perfect features. He wanted her to be sure. He'd always tried to do the right thing, but this time he was determined to get it right, no matter what that cost him.

Her blue eyes flashed with passion and nervousness, but no regrets. He kissed her softly and nearly lost it as her lips clung to his in unmistakable need.

"Why me?" he asked.

The question made her smile. "Why not you?"

"But I'm just a—"

She stopped him with a kiss. "No, you're not *just* anything. You're strong and safe. I like you and I trust you."

Her words made him feel ten feet tall and downright invincible. They also toppled about half the ice around his heart—ice formed by loneliness and a sense of having failed at his first marriage. She was more than a desirable woman to him; she was getting under his skin. If he had the sense God gave a snake, he would turn tail and run. Instead he reached for the second button on her dress and unfastened it.

He cleared his throat, trying not to notice the growing expanse of perfect, pale skin. "This is where I tell you that I'll stop anytime you'd like."

Despite her obvious apprehension, she gave him a faint smile. "Liar."

"Hey, I'm trying to be a gentleman."

"I think this would go better if you told me that you want me desperately and that you'll die if you don't have me."

"All of that is true."

"Really?"

At that moment, with her dress open to the sweet valley between her full breasts and her long auburn hair tumbling loose over her shoulders, she was both sultry and incredibly innocent looking.

"I've never wanted anyone the way I want you, Alex." He leaned close and pressed a kiss at the base of her collarbone. "I swear."

She clutched at him. He unfastened the rest of the buttons, then pushed the dress off her shoulders until the delicate wool puddled at her feet. She wore scraps of lace instead of a bra, and beneath her panty hose were the tiniest pair of panties he'd ever seen. Both in peach. Both more tempting than legal.

He swore under his breath as he stared at her curves, her pale skin, the rapid rise and fall of her chest. "If I'd known what you were wearing—or not wearing—under those conservative clothes of yours, I would have thrown you down on the sofa and had my way with you that first night."

She blushed and half raised her hands to cover her breasts. At that moment Mitch remembered that Alex hadn't had a whole bunch of experience with men. He wanted to ask how many she'd been with, but figured that was a surefire mood breaker. Instead he decided to treat her like a virgin. That way he'd go slow enough for her to relax.

He knelt on the floor and peeled down her panty hose, then had her sit on the edge of his bed. When he picked up one foot, she opened her mouth to no doubt ask him what on earth he was doing. Then he licked the inside of her ankle. Her eyes widened, then closed. A soft sound escaped her parted lips.

Moving a millimeter at a time, he kissed and licked his way up to the inside of her knee, then started on her other leg. When he'd repeated his action, he took her right hand in his and nibbled on the center of her palm. By the time he reached the inside of her elbow, she'd broken out in goose bumps, and her breathing had increased.

As he urged her to lie down, he pulled off his boots and socks, then stretched out next to her. "Pretty lady," he murmured before kissing her mouth.

She parted for him instantly. Their tongues stroked and circled, sending fire through him. He'd been hard for what felt like hours, but being next to her like this, knowing they were going to make love, sent even more blood south. His erection pulsed in time with his rapid heartbeat, and he had to concentrate to keep from rubbing himself against her. He wanted her more than he'd ever wanted a woman before in his life. He needed to be inside of her the way a drowning man needed to breathe.

He touched her shoulder, then brought his hand lower, cupping her breasts. The silky lace was smooth and cool against his hand. In the front seat of his truck he'd been too eager to touch her to even notice what kind of lingerie she wore. But now he took the time to tease her, tracing the top of the bra, barely touching her bare skin.

She wrapped her arms around his neck, pulling him close. He responded in kind, drawing her into his arms, then raising her up slightly so he could reach behind her and unfasten her bra. When he pulled the garment away, he broke their kiss so that he could look at her. Her tight nipples were the palest shade of peach.

"I know you taste as sweet as you look," he murmured just before taking that taut peak in his mouth.

She gasped as he suckled her, drawing her in, then gently, so gently, brushing his teeth against the small point. Her hips began to push against him, telling him that she was getting wet, swelling, preparing for him. As much as he wanted to rip off his clothes and bury himself inside of her, he deliberately slowed his pace even more. As he licked one breast, he cupped the other, his fingers and tongue working together to make her lose control.

"Mitch," Alex breathed as she tossed her head from side to side. She couldn't believe how good everything felt. For a few minutes she'd been so worried and nervous, but now she couldn't concentrate on anything but what he was doing to her body. His touches, the pressure of his body against her, the weight and strength of him. It all felt so right. She'd half expected a little voice to be whispering that this wasn't what she was supposed to be doing, but instead she was at peace. Well, as at peace as a woman in her condition could be.

An ache had taken residence between her legs. She recognized the symptoms from the time they'd been together in his truck. She wanted him to touch her there again and make her feel those things. She wanted to experience that ecstasy. It was like being transformed, or suddenly discovering that she could fly.

When his hand slipped down her stomach, she smiled and trembled in anticipation. When he pulled off her panties, she raised her hips so that she could help. But when he moved between her legs, she opened her eyes to look at him. What was he doing?

Mitch caught her gaze, then winked. "You're gonna love it," he promised, right before he bent down and kissed her right thigh.

She opened her mouth to protest, or at least question his actions. But while she was still figuring out what she was going to say, he parted the protective folds of her woman's place and licked her. She saw his head lower, followed by the flash of his tongue. Then she felt such a startling, intense jolt of pleasure and need and fire that all she could do was sink back on the bed, close her eyes and pray that he would never stop.

Her legs eased open. He licked her again, exploring, gently teasing until he found the one spot that had her surging against him. He was doing it again, making her feel those things. Only this time with his mouth and his tongue, not his fingers, and somehow that was better.

Hot sensations rolled through her, making her thighs shake and her breasts swell even more. Low in her belly, muscles tensed and released in time with his ministrations. He was slow and steady, building pressure inside of her. She remembered her climax the last time and how she hadn't been sure what to expect. This time the path seemed so much quicker. She was torn—wanting to take forever because the journey was so incredible, yet aching for her release.

He kissed and licked and sucked that one sensitive spot. Never too hard, never too fast, always exactly right. As if he could read her mind, or feel what she felt. Then, too soon it seemed, she felt her body collecting itself. Mitch felt it, too. He went faster and lighter, urging her on. She dug her heels into the mattress and raised her hips against his mouth.

"I want…" she breathed, unable to articulate what it was she wanted. She felt him smile. Then she couldn't think, couldn't do anything but feel the wonder of his touch. The passion-storm began deep inside of her and spiraled out. When it touched her most secret place, the explosion began. There was light and heat and a sense of drowning in the most perfect pool of well-being. She wanted to be swallowed up forever. She wanted always to be in this perfect state.

Then she was surfacing, and Mitch was holding her and kissing her face. "Sweet Alex," he murmured. "I knew you'd be like this."

"Like what?"

"Perfect. Just perfect."

He wrapped his arms around her and held her close. She rested her head on his shoulder and listened to the steady rhythm of his heartbeat. If wishes were possible, she would always want to be with this man, she thought contentedly. Here on the ranch, with the one person in the whole world who saw her as herself.

She could love him. Perhaps she already did. Alex kept her eyes closed in case he was watching her. She didn't want him to know what she was thinking. Love. Did she love Mitch? Alex probed her heart, searching for the truth. She respected him, she cared for him, her life was better since meeting him. He knew her better than most people did, even her family. He made her feel things she'd never felt before. If that was love, then she'd fallen for him. How ironic. After years of thinking she wasn't one for emotions or passion, she'd finally figured out she had plenty of both. She'd finally found where she belonged, and it was one place she could never stay.

A sense of pure sadness threatened to overwhelm her. Alex pushed the emotion away. Not yet. She would think about it later. For now they had each other and this time of magic and intimacy.

"What are you thinking?" he asked.

"That you're very good at what you do. You must

practice a lot." She risked opening her eyes and saw that her teasing had done what she'd hoped. She'd distracted him to the point that he wasn't going to probe.

"I do not practice," he growled. "I'll have you know I'm very selective about the women in my life. So much so that I've spent most of the past several years living like a monk."

"So you're probably not even interested in sex anymore."

His expression tightened with desire. "On the contrary, my naked little princess, I'm in a bad way. I have every intention of burying myself deep inside of you until you're so ready and hot, you'll beg."

"I would never beg."

"Wanna bet?"

The way he said it, she knew she would be begging before the night was out, and in an incredible way that she was going to remember forever. But for now it was enough to watch as he sat up and pulled off his shirt. When his hands dropped to his belt, Alex felt herself starting to blush. She'd never seen a man naked before, except for those shadowy glimpses they showed in the movies. When Mitch pushed down his jeans and briefs and his...well, his...manliness sprang forth, she thought she might very well start begging right now. She wanted to touch him and see if he felt soft or rough. But he didn't give her the chance.

"I promised myself I'd take it really slow," he said as he pulled open his nightstand drawer and removed a condom. "And I really want to. Except—" he stared at her "—you have no idea how much I need to be inside of you."

"I want that, too," she said, and meant it. She wanted to know and she wanted her first time to be with Mitch.

"I promise amazing technique and staying power next time."

She wasn't sure what he was referring to, but she smiled and nodded, then tried not to stare open-mouthed as he quickly and gracefully put on the protection. Then he was kneeling between her thighs, and she felt the pressure of his arousal against her slick wet opening.

Before she could tell him that she wasn't sure what she was supposed to do, he'd bent down and kissed her. With his tongue against hers and one hand stroking between her legs, she found not knowing what to do didn't seem so bad. Then he was pushing inside of her. Pushing and stretching and filling her.

The pressure didn't hurt, exactly, but it was unfamiliar. She told herself to relax. Because she'd been so active as a girl, she knew there wasn't going to be physical proof of her innocence. A doctor had warned her of that several years ago. So, with a little luck, Mitch would never know.

His hips flexed against hers and he gave a low grown. "You're so tight."

The way he said it, she assumed it was a good thing. Then he was moving in and out of her. The uncomfortable pressure decreased, but the good pressure, the kind she'd felt before when he'd touched her and kissed her down there, started. She found herself flexing against him, wanting him to thrust inside her more.

"I can't," he breathed against her mouth. "I can't hold back."

He broke their kiss and straightened slightly. He grabbed her hips and held her still while he buried himself inside of her over and over again. Their eyes locked. She watched his expression tighten. He swore. "I'm not going to last much longer."

In a flash of insight, she realized he was both warning her and asking for permission. "It's all right," she assured him, feeling the tingling inside of her grow. She realized that if they did it again and it took a little longer, she would climax herself.

He thrust inside deeper still, then froze in place. His mouth opened and his lips formed her name, but he didn't actually speak. She watched as the wave of pleasure crashed over him, making him first tense, then shudder. He collapsed against her, pulling her close, then rolling onto his side and taking her with him, their arms and legs wrapped around each other.

He was still buried inside of her. Alex inhaled the masculine scent of him and of their lovemaking. This was how it was supposed to be, she thought in contentment. She knew they would make love again and again, and each time it would be better.

"You're full of surprises," Mitch said, then kissed her forehead, her cheek and her nose.

Nothing in his tone warned her, so she was unprepared when he raised his head and stared at her, then spoke again.

"But you should have told me you were a virgin."

Chapter Fourteen

Alex's expression shifted swiftly, showing shock, then disbelief, then guilt. Until he'd seen the last emotion, Mitch had been praying he'd been wrong. But her sudden inability to meet his eyes warned him that his worst nightmare had just come true.

"How did you know?" she asked.

"I didn't," he said flatly. "It was a hunch. You just confirmed it."

"Oh."

"Yeah, oh."

He pulled out of her and rolled onto his back, then pressed the heels of his hands against his eyes. What the hell had he just done? Alex looked a few years younger, but he knew for a fact that she was pushing thirty. How could she still be a virgin? Then he remembered that she wasn't an ordinary woman—that she was royalty and that she'd been saving herself for Prince Charming.

"What gave me away?" she asked. "Did I do something wrong?"

He felt more than heard the quaver in her voice. Dammit. She was about to get all female on him and start worrying about whatever it was women worried about in this particular situation. When had everything spun out of control, and how could he undo what they'd just done?

Except he didn't want to. Mitch groaned low in his throat. That was the hell of it. Even if someone offered him a way back about thirty minutes, he wouldn't take it. Because for some stupid macho reason, he was glad that he'd been Alex's first time, which made as little sense as her wanting him to be the one to change her life.

He rolled over and faced her. Her auburn curls tumbled across the pillow. Her skin was impossibly pale, with a faint rose glow staining her face and her chest. It was the lingering physical manifestation of her release, and he was fiercely glad that he'd done that to her.

"It's your fault," he told her. "If you weren't so beautiful and so imperious, none of this would have happened. I'll be damned if I'll have regrets, but we both know we shouldn't have done that."

"Why not?"

"Because."

She smiled. "Oh, there's a sterling reason."

He touched her cheek, then rubbed his thumb across her mouth. "You make me crazy."

"In a good way?"

"In the best way possible." He lowered his hand into her hair and squeezed a fistful of curls. "So have I committed a felony or what? There have to be some pretty stiff penalties for stealing a royal princess's virtue."

"I'll have to do some research, but I have a fairly close relationship with the king, and I'm sure I can get him to go easy on you, as they say here in your country."

"Sorry, Alex, but the king isn't going to want to do much more than change me from a bull to a steer."

She thought about that for a second, then glanced down. "Oh, my. I see your point. That would be tragic."

"For me more than you."

They stared at each other. She drew in a deep breath. "Was it awful?"

"What? Making love with you?"

She nodded.

"Why would you think that?" he asked. "It was incredible."

"Then how did you know I was a virgin?"

"You were more tentative than I'd expected, and you seemed too startled to have done it before. But I wasn't sure." He grimaced. "And I was too much of a selfish bastard to make sure before I had my way with you."

Her blue eyes darkened. "So you're sorry?"

"Only for how it affects you. I've changed you, Alex, and you can never go back."

"I don't want to go back. I've been saving myself

for years, and I suddenly realized there wasn't much point. I'm not engaged. So far my parents show no signs of arranging a match for me. I refuse to die an old maid.''

''You're far from that.''

She turned toward him and rested her hand on his waist. ''I'm not sorry. I don't have any regrets. Given the choice, I would do it all again...with you.'' She moved closer, then lowered her hand and encircled him. ''Speaking of which.''

Her fingers were warm and tentative, but they were more than enough to get him hard again. He sucked in a breath. ''It's like being seventeen again.''

''Is that a bad thing?''

''Not if you don't mind doing it five or six times tonight.''

She smiled. ''That sounds like a good plan to me. I have a lot of catching up to do. I want to learn everything and I want you to be the one to teach me.'' She pressed her mouth to his.

He couldn't resist her kiss any more than he'd resisted her touch, or the woman herself. As he began touching her, a little voice whispered that he was in way over his head. But he ignored the words, much as he ignored the sensation of his heart opening up to this very special, very unavailable woman.

''Are you ready?'' Alex asked as the limo pulled in front of the Century City Hotel.

Mitch nodded without speaking. He would rather be dragged around a corral by an angry bull than admit that he was nervous...but he was. It wasn't every day that a man escorted a royal princess to a high-society event.

He and Alex were staying at a small, exclusive hotel in Malibu. Their suite took up the entire top level, and there were security people staying on the floor below. One of the royal bodyguard rode next to the driver in the limo, and there would be more security people—from both Wynborough and the United States Secret Service—at the fund-raiser tonight. Mitch had even been briefed on the proper etiquette for the evening.

The right rear door opened. As he'd been instructed, Mitch stepped out first, then assisted Alex. She straightened and smiled to the crowd. Instantly the evening exploded as dozens of flashes popped all around them. Mitch stayed in the background and was jostled and ignored as the press tried to get Alex's attention.

"What do you think of your stay in our country?"

"Where have you been hiding out, Princess Alexandra?"

"Have you met any Hollywood heartthrobs?"

Alex kept smiling, then took Mitch's arm and allowed him to lead her toward the entrance to the hotel. Mitch found that a firm right arm worked wonders in holding back the crowd. But there were too many people taking up too small a space. He was reminded of the time when he'd been eight and had fallen into a corral of milling steers. He'd been tossed and jostled until his dad had come to his rescue.

Just when he figured he'd had all he could take, they pushed through the last of the people and made it inside. The foyer of the hotel was open, well lit and relatively quiet.

A well-dressed man in his mid-thirties greeted them. ''Princess Alexandra, welcome to America. I'm Miles Stanford, an attaché with the State Department.'' He bent over Alex's hand, then straightened and smiled at Mitch. ''Mr. Colton, a pleasure.''

Mitch wasn't sure what to say, but Miles didn't wait for any greeting. He took Alex's arm and led her toward the ballroom, chatting all the way. Mitch trailed after them. There were dozens of women in fancy dresses partnered with tuxedo-clad men. The light sparkling off all the jewelry was enough to blind a person. Nothing about this event made him happy. He knew he was out of place and he figured just about everyone around them knew it, too. He should have waited back at their hotel.

Except Alex had asked him to come, and he hadn't wanted to disappoint her. If he was going to be honest with himself, he would also admit he wanted to spend as much time with her as possible. She wasn't going to be in his life forever, and when she was gone he would miss her. So rather than waste time, he would put up with the formalities and the State Department and even the press.

They entered the ballroom. There was an instant hush, followed by a burst of conversation. Mitch kept a few steps back as Alex was introduced to the waiting dignitaries. He saw the men watching her and the women talking about her, and he knew it wasn't all because she was royal. Some of it was because of how she looked.

They'd spent the past three days in bed, discovering each other. Although he knew every inch of her body and could reduce her to damp, quivering passion in about thirty seconds, he hadn't known she was a princess. Not really down-to-his-bones known, the way he had when she'd come out of their bathroom in their suite. In a matter of less than an hour, with some cosmetics, hot curlers and whatever magic it seemed women knew from birth, she'd transformed herself. He'd always thought she was hot and sexy, but she'd turned into stunning and regal, as well.

She wore a long, silk, strapless gown in deep red. The soft fabric clung to her curves, outlining the perfect shape of her body. The same fabric draped across her midsection and fell to the floor forming a kind of train. A diamond and ruby necklace with matching, dangling earrings caught the red of the dress and sparkled in the light. He figured there was enough carat weight around her neck alone to finance about ten thousand head of cattle. Her long, auburn hair had been piled high on her head in a riot of curls anchored in place with an honest-to-God tiara. The kind he'd only ever seen in pictures. She'd told him it was nearly four hundred years old and insured for six million dollars. Six *million* for headgear. Who would have thought? She wore long, red gloves and an antique-looking bracelet around her left wrist. He hadn't dared to ask the value of that bauble.

As the crowd pressed around them, Mitch found himself pushed farther away from Alex. In three-inch heels, she towered over many of the people around her, so it wasn't hard to keep her in view.

This would be, he realized, her husband's lot in life. Once, she'd talked about the special characteristics necessary for a man to function as partner to a princess. The situation would be worse if Alex became queen of her country. Mitch stepped back and walked over to the bar, ordered himself a drink, then leaned against one of the room's pillars.

Dozens of tables had been set up for an elaborate dinner. There was a huge dance floor, a full orchestra and a podium. Mitch had already listened to Alex practice her speech that afternoon. They'd edited it a couple of times, then gone over it until she was comfortable with the material. She was a natural at public speaking. His gaze settled on her deft handling of the mass of people around her. She was good at a lot of things.

He was going to have a hell of a time letting her go, he thought grimly. She'd become the best part of his world. His feelings had gone way beyond liking, but he wasn't going to waste any time exploring what else they might be. He knew his place, and it was in Arizona, not Wynborough. Not that she was making him any offers.

But he found he couldn't tear his gaze away from her face as she spoke with the various people being introduced to her. Nor could he help smiling and winking when she glanced up, searched the room, then visibly relaxed when her gaze met his. She gave a tiny shrug as if to say this couldn't be helped. He nodded in return. He knew she had to do her thing, and when she was finished, he would go to her. After all, she'd promised him the first dance.

* * *

"You're kidding," he said two hours later as the orchestra started playing.

Alex shook her head. "I'm sorry, Mitch. I thought you understood."

He glanced around at the several hundred people in the huge ballroom. When he'd jokingly asked her for the first dance, he hadn't realized that as the guest of honor, she and her escort would be dancing together...alone...on display.

"Guess I should have paid more attention at those dance lessons," he said.

She brightened. "You took lessons?"

"No. That was a joke. But I'll muddle through."

Just like he'd muddled through the rest of the evening. After about thirty minutes of mingling, one of the State Department folks had led him to Alex's side where he'd had the privilege of escorting her to dinner. There, he'd made polite conversation with a senator and his wife, and the lieutenant governor of California. Not bad for a rancher and former rodeo rider.

"You're hating this," Alex murmured as he pulled back her chair, then led her onto the dance floor.

"Not at all."

She sighed, then stepped into his arms. "You are. I can tell. You have this scrunchy expression around your eyes."

Mitch laughed. "Scrunchy? Is that a royal word?"

"No, but I understand these things can be a royal pain. You've been very understanding, and I appreciate that. I'm sorry we were separated earlier, but that happens. I have so many people I have to talk with."

"I understand," he told her. "You ran me through the drill before we got here, so there weren't any surprises. I'm not mad. Quit worrying."

She was standing so close that it was easy to move with her. The music had a steady beat, and after a couple of circles around the dance floor, other couples joined them.

Her gaze was steady. "I really appreciate you doing this for me."

"I know. It's fine."

"I mean it."

"Alex." He growled her name. "Let it go. I want to be here, because I want to be with you."

She leaned close and pressed her mouth to his ear. "I want to be with you, too, but I think it would cause something of a scandal if we did it right here on the dance floor. So let's wait until we get back to the room."

Her words aroused him. He tried to think neutral thoughts so that his body wouldn't respond in an obvious and predictable manner. The last thing he needed was to get a lecture from Miles on the impropriety of getting a hard-on while dancing with a foreign dignitary.

"We've been doing 'it' as you call making love several times a day. Aren't you tired of it yet?" he asked.

She laughed. "No. I'll never be tired of you touching me or being inside of me."

His teasing had backfired, and her words had created images that were damn hard to ignore.

"You're killing me, darlin'," he said.

"But in a good way."

"The best."

They smiled at each other. He wanted to kiss her, but he knew he couldn't. Later, he promised himself. Later he would kiss her all over, loving her until they were both—

A flash of light exploded in his face. "Mr. Colton, how did you meet the princess?"

Mitch glanced up and saw a reporter standing next to him. The young man motioned for his photographer to get another shot.

"This is a private function," Mitch said, staying calm even though all he wanted to do was shove the punk out of the way. Instead he turned his back on him.

"You're her escort for the evening," the man persisted. "Are you more than friends? Is this a romantic relationship?"

From the corner of his eye he saw several groups of security heading their way. But they weren't going to get there quickly enough. More flashes popped in his face. Alex ducked her head.

"What do you want to do?" Mitch asked softly. "Should I lead you away?"

"No. I refuse to run. Just ignore him."

"Mr. Colton, don't you want to clarify your relationship with Princess Alexandra?"

Mitch turned to the man, who was all of five-seven or five-eight. He could have squashed the guy like a bug. "You don't want to know what I want to do, kid, because it would involve a lot of pain for you."

The reporter opened his mouth, but before he could

ask another question, security arrived and grabbed him and his photographer, then dragged them from the room.

Alex was grinning at him. "You were so macho," she said. "You threatened him."

"It wasn't a threat. It was a statement of fact."

She laughed. "Oh, Mitch. There aren't many men like you, and I think that's sad."

He pulled her close. "You're just jealous because I'm the better dancer."

"That's true." She rested her head on his shoulder. "You do realize that there are going to be more reporters when we leave. Chances are by this time next week, you're going to see pictures of yourself plastered over the front of tabloids."

He hadn't realized. He hadn't given the press a moment's thought. "Well, hell," he muttered. "At least my mother will be thrilled. She's been complaining for years that she doesn't have a current picture of me."

Chapter Fifteen

"I'm almost afraid to ask," Alex said as she settled on the sofa in their suite. "But what did you think?"

Mitch slowly loosened his tie and pulled it free of his collar, then sat next to her. He'd removed his tuxedo jacket when they returned back from the party. His shoes had quickly followed. Now he was unfastening the first couple of buttons of his shirt. She hadn't really thought of the slightly rumpled, not-quite-undressed look as being sexy, but she found herself wanting to reach over and kiss him until they were making love.

Instead, she stayed in her corner of the small couch. For reasons she wasn't willing to explore right now, she needed to know how he'd survived the evening. Had he hated it so much that he would never want to do it again, or had it been not as awful as he'd first thought?

Mitch angled toward her, then leaned forward and patted her leg. "I survived. It was different than I'd imagined," he admitted. "I guess I didn't let myself think about it too much. It's not the sort of situation anyone would walk into willingly. You did warn me that I would be ignored for the first part of the evening, then surrounded for the second. You were right."

Alex bit back a sigh. She'd been afraid that once the press figured out her escort was a tall, good-looking rancher no one had heard of, the speculation would begin. While their trip from the car to the hotel had been relatively uneventful, their short walk back, at the end of the evening, had been a nightmare of paparazzi and yelled questions.

"Telling me you survived doesn't exactly answer my question," she said.

"What do you want to know, princess?" he asked. "Did I like it? No. Is that how I want to live my life? Not for any amount of money. Could I deal with it infrequently? Probably. I've lived through worse with the stomach flu."

Despite her concerns, Alex had to laugh. "I'm sure the organizers of the fund-raiser will be thrilled to know that you compare their event to a case of severe stomach upset."

"You know what I mean."

"Actually, I do. It's easy for me to talk about the visibility of my situation and all that I'm expected to do for my country, but it's quite another to live it firsthand.'' She leaned her head against the sofa. ''In an odd way, I share your feelings. I've been at the ranch for several weeks now, and I've grown used to the quiet and privacy. While I had a good time talking with everyone, I did find myself looking forward to returning to Arizona.''

''I'm glad,'' Mitch said, and took her hand in his.

She studied their clasped fingers. A week ago the thought of him doing this would have made her hyperventilate. But since Wednesday they'd been lovers. She smiled as she thought of the word. *Lovers.* She had a man in her life. And not just any man, but someone wonderful. Someone she trusted.

Tonight, at the table, she'd been proud to be with Mitch. Whether speaking to a senator or the table server, he'd been polite, at ease and charming. She'd caught several women eyeing him, wondering who he was and if he was available. She'd found herself wishing it could all be real.

''You're looking serious about something,'' he said. ''A kiss for your thoughts.''

''I thought the saying was a penny.''

''It is, but I figured I'd get more action with a kiss.''

She met his dark gaze and found herself very willing to get lost there. ''You would be right.'' She squeezed his hand. ''I was thinking about tonight, and about my time on the ranch. When my sisters and I decided to come to your country, I thought that when we'd discovered the truth about our brother and returned home I would be glad to go. I never thought I could be happy anywhere else.''

"Are you happy at the ranch?"

"Very. My few weeks of being normal have reminded me that I'm more than a princess. I'm also a woman. Between my duties and my responsibilities, I seemed to have forgotten that. My stay here has shown me I need to make time for normalcy. I suspect other women have had to deal with this, as well."

"With being a princess? I don't think so, darlin'. That would be your specialty."

"Oh, it's not exactly the same, but I was thinking about the question of working outside the home, or staying home to raise children. The traditional role versus what one actually wants and what one feels is right. There are also economic factors. My questions are different. How do I balance what is right for me and what is right for the country?"

"I have to admit, Alex, I can't see you staying home and changing diapers for some guy working swing shift at a factory."

His voice was teasing. She tucked her left foot under her and nodded. "I would guess you're right. I would hate my husband working swing shift. He could never accompany me to any social events." Her humor faded. "I know that I would have to do more than just stay home. If I wasn't living in Wynborough and handling my responsibilities there, I would need to be involved on a local level."

"Politics?"

"Never. I was thinking more of charity work. I was raised to believe I must give back. My sisters and I have been very blessed. We've been taught that blessings come with responsibilities."

"I thought princesses only married princes. Isn't there one in waiting?"

There wasn't and she was grateful. She couldn't imagine any man in her life but Mitch. "As you may have noticed, princes are in short supply. These days we're expected to marry well, but not into royalty. I would prefer a prince of a man. A good man whom I could respect. Someone...special."

She found herself unable to meet his gaze. She wanted to know what he was thinking, but she didn't dare ask. The conversation was incredibly general, skirting around important personal issues. Did she want to press for more? Did she have the courage? After all, it wasn't as if she had any answers. She knew that she cared about Mitch very much. She would miss him when she was gone, perhaps more than she realized.

"You deserve someone special," he told her. "And if the guy ever treats you badly, you tell me and I'll go beat him up."

She knew he meant his comment to be funny, but Alex found herself suddenly fighting tears. "You are so good to me," she murmured, and leaned against him. Mitch pulled her close, wrapping her in his strong arms.

Home, she thought as she closed her eyes. Here she was home.

Mitch knew he was in trouble. He'd known it the moment Alex had driven her fancy-pants car onto his ranch and he'd ignored the feeling. Unfortunately it had only grown over time. Now he was in too deep and there wasn't a damn thing he could do about it.

All he could do was hold her tight and not think about how lonely it was going to be when she was gone.

He wanted to believe what she'd said—that she wasn't looking for a prince, but instead wanted a prince of a man. Mitch knew he had some good qualities and some bad ones. Measured against most of the world, he thought he might come out okay. Except Alex wouldn't measure him against the rest of the world. As much as he wanted to forget the truth, he couldn't. She was a princess. Her father was a king. The man ran a country. Was he, Mitch, going to marry into royalty? Yeah, right. Even if Alex didn't end up inheriting the throne, which he really couldn't think about, who wanted a king as a father-in-law? What would he say when they had her folks over for dinner? What would he buy everyone for Christmas? Speaking of which, he said, "It's only a few weeks until Christmas. What are your plans?"

Alex looked at him. "I don't know. I really want to stay in the area until John returns, but I'm already intruding. Would you like me to stay at a hotel?"

"No. I want you to stay with me, for as long as you'd like."

Her blue eyes darkened. She kissed him. "Thank you. That's what I want, too. To stay with you."

Forever, he thought, and then he knew. This had gone beyond caring, beyond friendship and affection. Somehow, without meaning to, even knowing it to be the most stupid thing he'd ever done, he'd fallen in love with Princess Alexandra of Wynborough.

He drew her onto his lap and held her close, rocking her gently. "I want you, Alex," he murmured.

"I want you, too."

She wrapped her arms around his neck and pressed her lips to his. While he responded, he knew that wasn't what he'd meant when he told her he wanted her. Of course he was desperate to make love with her again and again, for as long as they had together, but what he wanted was her...forever. He wanted her in his life. He wanted to wake up next to her every morning. He wanted to marry her and watch her grow round with their babies. He even wanted to figure out how to blend their two very different lives.

He wanted not to think about how empty his life was going to be when she was gone. Because he knew he couldn't ask her to stay. What could he possibly offer her that she couldn't get better somewhere else? What right did he have to so change her life?

So he didn't say anything. Instead he let his body speak his longing, his love and his pain. He took her into the bedroom and closed the door. Then he made love to her as if they might never have another night together.

Alex had barely taken her seat at her desk Monday morning when the phone rang. "Hello?" she answered.

"So, tell me all about Mitch Colton," her mother instructed. "He's very handsome and you look good together. Is he a skilled dancer?"

Alex didn't know whether to laugh or scream. It had been less than forty-eight hours since the fundraiser. "When did you get the pictures?"

"This morning. They were delivered with my coffee. I must tell you, seeing my oldest daughter so very happy was a lovely way to start my day. My only complaint is that you didn't phone to tell me you were in love. That's not the sort of thing I want to find out from a third party.''

Alex swallowed hard. "I'm not in love."

"Oh, Alexandra, save those lines for the press. It's as plain as day in these pictures. My goodness, the way he's holding you and you're looking at each other. It quite reminds me of my courtship with your father. It's very romantic. Now tell me everything."

"There's nothing to tell. We're good friends. I'm staying on his ranch. He's kind to me."

"Kind? I do not want to hear that this handsome cowboy is just kind. I refuse to believe he hasn't tried to seduce you. And if you tell me you've resisted too strongly, I'm going to be most disappointed."

"Mother!"

Her mother sighed. "Alexandra, don't be too good all the time. Life is short."

"I know. We're, um, well, we have become close."

"Are we talking about confidences over a stamp collection or are you using a euphemism for sex?"

Alex writhed in her chair. "I can't believe I'm having this conversation with my mother."

"And I can't believe you're such a prude."

"I'm not a prude. Yes, we're lovers. There, are you happy?"

"That's the wrong question. The right question is, Are *you* happy?"

Alex closed her eyes. She thought about yesterday,

which she and Mitch had spent on the beach at Malibu. Los Angeles had been experiencing one of its Indian summer days, with temperatures near eighty. They'd walked in the sand, laughed, then gone back to their room and made love again.

"Yes, Mother, I'm very happy. Mitch is a special man. He's everything you would want him to be, but most important, he sees me for myself. When I'm with him, I feel at ease and very safe."

Her mother sighed. "I understand completely. I wish you both all the best."

Alex didn't like the sound of that. "It's not what you're thinking, though. I don't love him."

"Really? Why not?"

Alex opened her mouth, but couldn't think of a single thing to say. They were talking about Mitch. It could never work between them. "I have my duty," she managed at last.

"It does always come down to that, doesn't it," her mother said. "Your father and I wanted you and your sisters to find your own way. That's why we never arranged matches for the four of you. True love is a rare and special thing. However, if after all this time you haven't found it, perhaps it's not in the cards for you. Maybe we should look into finding you a suitable husband. If that's what you want."

"I—I've always expected to marry for my country," Alex said slowly. "I planned to respect my husband. I had hoped love would come with time."

She was only saying what she'd thought a thousand times before, but for some reason the statements made her uncomfortable. Even as she spoke, a voice in her head screamed that she wanted more than duty and respect. She wanted love and passion. Did she really think she could marry another man and let him touch her the way Mitch touched her? Alex shuddered. How repulsive.

"I have to go," she told her mother. "I have to..." She stumbled over an excuse.

"That's all right, Alexandra. I understand. Your father and I will be in touch. Take care."

"Yes. You, too."

She didn't remember hanging up the phone, but when next she became aware of her surroundings, she found herself staring out the window at the paddock. Several horses raced back and forth in the bright morning light. At first this view had been unfamiliar, but now she knew each tree, each bush and the way the color of the sky would change with the movement of the sun from east to west. She'd always found it beautiful, but today the vista was restful as well.

The phone rang. She turned to face it, but didn't move from her spot. After three more rings, the answering machine clicked on. She heard her message, then a squeal that could only come from Serena.

"Alex, are you there?" her sister asked. "We've seen the pictures and we all think he's very yummy. And here we thought you were in Arizona actually searching for James. I can't believe you've found a man. Call us back and plan to tell everything. Bye."

The machine had barely stopped recording when the phone rang again. This time she recognized her sister Katherine's voice. "Alex, I'm guessing you're avoiding calls, which I don't blame you. I heard about the pictures.''

There was a slight pause and Alex imagined her sensible sister smiling. ''Who would have thought you'd find a handsome cowboy when we were supposed to be looking for our brother? I think I'm the tiniest bit jealous.'' Katherine laughed. ''Anyway, I wanted to phone and say 'well done,' then let you know that the infamous Bill Lewis has gone missing. I'm going to speak with his partner, Trey Sutherland, to find out what he knows.'' She laughed again. ''I feel a bit like a spy, sleuthing out clues. If this princess bit ever gets boring, I believe I might have a career as a detective.''

Alex smiled as well. Who would have thought their time in the States would have changed them so much? If Alex had taken a lover and Katherine was considering a career as a detective, she could only imagine what Serena would get out of her visit.

''That's all,'' Katherine said, obviously preparing to hang up.

Alex moved across the room and picked up the phone. ''I'm here,'' she said. ''You're right, I'm hiding out. I've already heard from mother and Serena.''

''The press won't be far behind,'' Katherine warned.

''First they have to find me.'' Alex twisted the phone cord around her fingers. ''So you're off to where?''

''New Mexico. As I said, no one has seen Bill Lewis in a while. His partner should be able to send me in the right direction.

"Are you all right with this?" Alex asked. "Do you want me to send Elizabeth with you?"

Katherine sighed. "I believe I can handle an interview with a businessman, thank you very much. I'll be fine."

"I worry," Alex said.

"As I worry about you."

"Be careful," Alex told her. "Let me know what you find out."

"I promise to do both. After all, I'm the sensible sister, remember? If you want to lose sleep over anyone, try Serena. You wouldn't believe the things she's threatening to do. Someone needs to lock her up."

Alex laughed. "I'll write a memo. Take care."

"Bye."

Alex heard a soft click as her sister hung up the phone. She replaced the receiver. It rang as soon as it rested in the cradle. Alex ignored the call. Instead she grabbed her jacket and ran from the room.

Fifteen minutes later she had Princess on a lead line and was exercising the mare at a slow trot. The activity was enough to keep her hands busy, but her mind still raced. She replayed her mother's conversation and tried to make sense of all that had happened in the past few weeks.

Was she in love with Mitch? Is that what had happened? But she couldn't have fallen for him. He was all wrong for her, or at the very least, he was complicated. They lived in different countries, they wanted different things. Or did they? She knew she wanted a caring partner and a family. Were Mitch's dreams so very far from that?

"It doesn't matter," she said aloud. "I have my duty to worry about."

Her duty. That was part of the problem, she realized. What was her duty? If they found her brother alive, then he would be heir to the throne. But what if they didn't? She felt there was a good chance that parliament would change the law, which meant she would be queen of her country. That would change her life entirely. As just one of four princesses, she would have more freedom in choosing her mate and her place of residence, but as queen, she would be limited by location, if nothing else. She couldn't live on a ranch. Besides, even if she could adjust, what about Mitch? He wasn't the kind of man who would wear the weight of being a consort well.

Alex stood in the center of the corral, holding the lead line and turning slowly as the mare trotted around her. She looked at the beautiful mountains, the house and the barn, at the well-kept grounds. This ranch had been in Mitch's family for generations. He wouldn't want to leave it. She would never ask him to. So there was no point in worrying about their feelings because it would never work. Except...

Alex groaned in frustration. She couldn't decide if she was being practical or a coward. Did she choose duty over love because duty was always clearer and safer? Did she love Mitch? Did he care about her? Were they having a torrid affair, or was it something more? If only she had the experience to know. But she didn't and she couldn't think of a single person to ask.

Princess slowed to a walk, then moved toward her.

When the mare snuffled at her jacket pocket, Alex pulled out a slice of apple and fed it to her.

"Sweet girl," she murmured, patting her neck, then stroking her soft nose. "You're getting more relaxed, aren't you? I missed you while I was gone. I think you missed me a little, too. Maybe by the end of the week you'll feel safe enough to let me ride you. Would that be nice?"

The bay mare nodded her head, as if she could understand. The thought made Alex smile. She hugged the horse. "Once I can ride you, it's just a matter of time until you're calm enough to breed again. Won't that be nice? You can have pretty babies of your own."

She closed her eyes and pressed her face into Princess's warm, sweet-smelling coat. The horse made a huffing sound. Alex took that as agreement. But when she tried to imagine the horse with her foals, what she saw instead were towheaded toddlers running through a field. Babies, but the human kind. Her children. Hers with Mitch.

A sharp jolt of longing wrapped itself around her heart. The unexpected pain made her gasp, and she bit her lower lip to keep from crying. Her mother had been right. She loved Mitch.

Maybe it would have been obvious to anyone but her. Maybe if she'd had more experience she would have recognized the symptoms. But she hadn't, and now it was too late. What was she supposed to do? How could she make it work? Because that was what she wanted. But did Mitch? She wasn't just the girl next door. If he felt the same way, they were going to have to do a lot of compromising. Was he willing to do that?

She imagined the sweet toddlers again and felt a smile tugging at her lips. They could have children together. Dozens of them. She laughed out loud. All right, perhaps not dozens, but at least two or—

Babies, she thought. Babies as in... A thought formed. Alex pushed it away, but it returned. She touched her flat stomach. She was fine, she told herself. She and Mitch had been very careful about using condoms. Her mind flashed back to the time they'd made love in the huge bathtub in his bathroom. That night things had gotten a little out of control, and neither of them had thought about protection. The same thing had happened twice in their suite in Malibu. But two or three times without birth control didn't mean anything. At least, she hoped it didn't.

Alex led the mare back to the barn. She wouldn't think about it, she told herself. She couldn't. Didn't she and Mitch have enough to deal with already without worrying about her being pregnant?

Chapter Sixteen

Okay, he was fifteen different kinds of a bastard. He knew that. The problem was that Alex probably knew it, too. Mitch paused outside of the den where he knew she was reading. He'd heard her walk by less than fifteen minutes before. He'd also heard her steps hesitate when she'd been in front of his office. He'd sensed her indecision as clearly as if she'd spoken aloud to him. He'd been able to read her thoughts. She wanted to know what was wrong.

In the past few days since they'd returned from Los Angeles, he'd alternated between completely avoiding her and being unable to get enough of her. During the day he stayed busy with work, twice not even coming back in time for dinner. But each night he'd appeared at her door, not saying anything, yet silently begging for admission. Each time he'd expected her to tell him what a jerk he was, or at the very least to slap him. Instead she'd led him to her bed. Each time he promised himself he was going to tell her the truth, or at least as much of it as he'd figured out. Which wasn't much.

But he hadn't. Instead he'd continued to bury himself in work because it was safe. Because he didn't feel that he had any choice in the matter. Because he didn't want to admit the truth.

He'd fallen for her. Not just in a casual, isn't-the-sex-great-and-maybe-we-can-get-together-some-time kind of way, but for real. As in wanting it all.

He swore softly. He'd made some mistakes in his life, but this was one of the biggest. Falling for a princess—what the hell had he been thinking? Except he hadn't been thinking, at least not with his head. He should have kept things light, or at the very least not bothered to find out there was an intriguing person behind the title. Life had been a whole lot easier when she'd gotten on his nerves.

If she'd been any other woman, he would have tried to make it work. He would have wanted to talk about compromise and kids and forever. But how was he supposed to compromise with a future queen? Was he willing to give up the ranch?

Mitch pressed his hand against the sturdy hall wall—the same wall his grandfather had built. His family had lived on this land for generations. Of course, Alex could make a case that hers had lived in Wynborough longer. In the grand scheme of things, what difference did his cattle ranch make? She might one day rule a country. Except his ranch mattered to him. He couldn't exist just to be her consort. He didn't have any answers, which was why he'd been avoiding her.

"Talk about putting the cart before the horse," he muttered. "You don't even know how she feels about you."

It was true, he realized. She might think he was a lot of fun for the moment, but no more permanent than a summer—or in this case winter—romance. There was only one way to find out. He pushed open the door and stepped into the study.

Alex sat curled up in one of the big wing chairs flanking the stone fireplace. The green leather was the perfect foil for her coloring. Her hair glowed as bright as the flames in the hearth. She glanced up when he entered. Her eyes were dark and unreadable, her expression pleasant but wary. In the past couple of days he'd given her no reason to trust him or welcome him. If things had gone badly, he only had himself to blame.

"Can I interrupt?" he asked.

"Of course."

She closed her book and placed it on the small table next to her chair. He took the seat opposite hers and wondered how he was supposed to begin. "I have some news," he said. "I don't know whether to tell you it's good or bad. I guess that depends on how you interpret it."

She raised her eyebrows, but didn't say anything.

"My parents called a little earlier," he said. "A reporter tracked them down and wanted to interview them about our relationship. When they claimed not to know anything, the guy showed them pictures.'' He gave her a slight smile. ''The ones they took at the dance.''

''Yes, my parents saw those, as well.''

''I can't figure out what the big deal is,'' Mitch told her. ''We were just dancing. Anyway, my mother called to let me know that she and my father would be flying in to meet you.''

Alex stiffened. ''Your parents want to meet me?'' She sounded horrified.

''It's all right. You're a princess. I'm sure you'll do fine.''

She shook her head. ''I do much better with a group of five hundred than one-on-one. At least in situations like that. I've never met a man's parents before.''

''All the princes you know are orphans?''

She glared at him. ''That's not what I meant, and you know it. I've never met the parents of the man I was, well, involved with.''

Despite all that they were going to have to talk about, he couldn't help teasing her. ''You mean your lover's parents.''

''Yes. Thank you for making that so clear. My lover's parents.''

He leaned back in the chair. ''You'll do fine. You're pretty, intelligent, you have a great job. What's not to like?''

She smiled. ''When you put it like that, I sound like a prize.''

''You *are* a prize, Alex.'' His momentary humor faded. ''They'll get here in the next couple of days.

They wouldn't tell me exactly when. They hadn't booked their flights when they called, and they don't want us to bother taking time off to pick them up. My parents are like that.''

''How lovely.'' She closed her eyes briefly. ''I'm taking up two guest rooms. Is that going to be a problem? Is there enough room?''

''Plenty.''

She nodded. ''How long will they stay?''

''I don't know. A few days. They haven't been back in nearly a year, but they won't want to be away from their bed-and-breakfast for long.''

He crossed one ankle over the opposite knee and tried to relax. But the knot in his gut wasn't going anywhere and all he could think about was how empty his life would be when she was gone.

''We have to talk,'' he said.

She looked at him. ''I know.'' She tried a smile, but it failed pretty miserably. ''Things have gotten out of hand, haven't they? At least they have for me. I didn't mean to presume—'' she bit her lower lip ''—that is to say...''

''I know what you're getting at,'' he told her, then tried a fake smile of his own. ''I didn't know you'd start to matter so much. We've created an impossible situation.''

She shifted in her chair. ''More than impossible. Potentially disastrous.''

''What?''

She looked startled, as if she hadn't meant to speak aloud. ''There are ramifications that neither of us considered.''

What was she going on about? "The press?" he asked.

"That, too."

"Alex, you're not making any sense."

"I know. I don't think I want to." She stood up and crossed to stand next to him. "Mitch, I don't want to talk about this right now. I'm confused and frightened and all I want is for you to hold me. Let's worry about the rest of it tomorrow."

He wasn't sure he wanted things put off. He'd worked himself up to having this conversation with her and he wanted it done. He wanted to put his cards on the table and tell her that he loved her. But he couldn't resist her invitation.

He rose to his feet and pulled her close. "But tomorrow we talk," he said.

"Yes. I need to go into town in the morning, then we'll talk after that."

"What's in town?" he asked, his voice teasing. "You want to check out the other cowboys to see if you can do better?"

Instead of answering with a laugh or a comment of her own, she wrapped her arms around him and hung on as if she never wanted to let go. "You don't know how much I need you," she whispered.

He felt an answering tug in his own heart, and the whisper of the pain to come. "Actually, I do."

They didn't make it into town until later the next afternoon. One of the horses had turned up lame and they'd spent the morning tending to the injured animal.

''Thanks for your help with Midnight,'' Mitch said as they drove into Hope.

''You're more than welcome. I really like working with the horses. They seem so much less complicated than the rest of the world.''

''I know what you mean.''

Their conversation fizzled into silence, as it had continually since they'd climbed into his truck. What was going on? he wondered. Last night had been— he shook his head not sure how to describe the previous evening. When they'd walked into his bedroom, it was as if they suddenly couldn't get enough of each other. While their lovemaking was usually intense, last night they'd barely taken the time to get undressed before falling into bed. He'd needed her so much and his passion and desire had been more than matched by hers. Again and again she'd reached for him, arousing him with her hands and her mouth, making him hard and ready over and over again. They'd barely slept. But this morning when he'd awakened, Alex had already left to return to her own bed. The chilly sheets on her side of the mattress had been an ugly reminder of his future without her.

''Where to?'' he asked as he drove down the main street.

''The drugstore,'' she said, pointing to the low building on the far corner. ''Just park in front. I'll only be a minute.''

He started to protest, to tell her that he would come inside with her, but she looked faintly embarrassed. He figured she had to buy some female stuff and didn't need him along for that.

When he parked, she slipped out of the cab and hurried into the store. He stared after her. They had to talk, he reminded himself. One of them had to be willing to say it first. Mitch decided he was going to be the one. As soon as she got back, he was going to flat out tell her that he loved her and then let her take it from there. He wasn't a prince, he wasn't sure he was anything close to a prince of a man, but he knew that no one could care about Alex the way he did. There had to be a way to make it work between them. He didn't want to face a lifetime of a cold, empty bed.

She returned in a matter of minutes. When she slid in beside him, she clutched the plastic bag to her chest. "I have to tell you something." She wasn't looking at him. Instead she stared straight ahead.

"What?"

"My parents are flying out to meet you."

A rock hit the pit of his stomach. Mitch wondered if this was how Alex had felt when he'd made his announcement last night. "Okay. When do they arrive?"

"I don't know. It's supposed to be a surprise, but Laura took pity on me this morning and phoned to tell me."

"So we'll have both sets of parents to deal with. That will be interesting. I've never met a king before." He had to swallow hard. "Betty will be thrilled to be cooking for more royalty."

"There's more," Alex said, glancing at him out of the corner of her eye. "I'm sorry, Mitch." She reached into the bag and pulled out a tabloid. A picture of them dancing together filled the front page. The caption above read "The Princess and the Cowboy. Royalty Finds Love in the American West."

He swore.

"My thoughts exactly. Every tabloid out has a similar headline. I'm really sorry. I didn't think this would happen when I invited you to the fund-raiser. If I had, I wouldn't have bothered you."

He didn't know what to say. All his life he'd lived just like everyone else, going about his business without worrying that the rest of the world would intrude. But this was different. He studied the color photograph. Alex looked incredibly beautiful, and he had to admit they looked good together. But this was his personal life on display.

"You're angry," she said.

"I'm in shock. There's a difference."

"You're not happy about it."

"Of course not. Who would be?"

She sighed. "I'm sorry."

He tossed down the paper. "Stop saying that. It's not your fault. You can't control what those jackals do."

"I know, but..."

He pulled her close and kissed the top of her head. "Don't sweat it, princess. We'll be fine."

"Will we? I worry about that. I worry about so many things."

"Leave the worrying to me. I have bigger shoulders so I can carry a bigger load. Okay, let's see what the other headlines say."

He reached for her plastic bag. It slipped easily out

of her hands, but then she made a grab for it. "No!" she cried.

Mitch was so startled he released it, but it was too late. The slick material draped across her lap, and slowly the contents slipped onto the cab floor. There were three more tabloids and a white box. He stared at the box, at the words printed on the side, then he looked at Alex. Her cheeks flamed with color.

He thought about the times they'd been careless— no, that *he'd* been careless because he'd wanted her so much. He thought about her wanting to talk. He returned his gaze to the home pregnancy test. "You're pregnant," he said.

She stared at him helplessly. "That's what we're going to find out."

The next morning they both looked at the plus sign on the stick. Alex didn't know whether to laugh or cry. For a moment she wished she were the fainting kind. A few minutes of oblivion would be very nice right now.

"Well, I'll be," Mitch said.

She felt her eyes fill up with tears. Until that moment she hadn't realized she'd been hoping for a more positive response from him. Yes, this was a complication neither of them expected, but it wasn't as if it was her fault. She walked into his bedroom and sat on the bed.

"You should have been more careful," she said, blinking away the tears. "You were the experienced one."

"Thanks for the news flash." He came after her,

stopping less than two feet in front of her. ''But it's not real helpful right now.''

''But making love without protection was irresponsible. You can't be that way.''

''I'm not usually. Things got out of hand for both of us. You're a very sexy woman and I wanted you. I won't apologize for that.''

''Fine. Make it my fault.'' She knew she was snapping at him for no reason, but she couldn't help it. Everything was so out of control. How had this all happened? How were they going to fix it? And why wasn't Mitch taking her in his arms and telling her that it was going to be all right?

''What's wrong with you?'' He stared down at her. ''Alex, you're not making any sense. If you want to say it's my fault, then it's my fault, but that doesn't deal with the problem.''

''Oh, so it's a problem now, is it? Then let it be my problem. I'm sorry you know about the baby.''

She started to stand up. He took her arm and held her in place. ''What's wrong with you?''

''Nothing.'' But she couldn't look at him. She couldn't let him see her eyes and guess the truth.

Unfortunately Mitch knew her too well. ''You're scared,'' he said, pulling her close. He wrapped his strong arms around her and held her tight. ''You don't know what to do and that terrifies you.''

''I'm perfectly fine,'' she lied.

He kissed the top of her head. ''Darlin', we're going to get through this together.''

''But this isn't how I planned on getting pregnant.''

"It's not how I planned on proposing to you, either, but here we are."

She raised her head and stared at him. Her heart stopped. Actually stopped. She heard it beat, then there was only silence. "You want to marry me?"

A slow smile curved his perfect mouth. "Haven't we already decided that you're a hell of a catch? Given the way I feel about you, I'd be a fool to let you go."

She couldn't believe it! "We're getting married?"

"Who's getting married?"

Alex looked up and saw two couples standing in the doorway to the bedroom. She knew her own parents and recognized Mitch's parents from the photos she'd seen in the family room.

Betty ducked around them. "Sorry," she said with an apologetic shrug. "They arrived within minutes of each other. I tried to keep them busy in the living room, but you guys were kind of yelling at each other, and they just followed the voices." She glanced at Alex's father. "Is he really a king?"

"I am, madam," King Phillip said, his bearing as regal as ever. He winked. "Pretty impressive, don't you think?"

With his white hair, neat beard and mustache, he looked like a Hollywood casting director's dream for the role of elder statesman. Normally Alex would be thrilled to see both him and her mother, but the realization that they had heard part or all of her argument with Mitch, not to mention the fact that she was pregnant, was too mortifying for words.

"I can't believe this," Alex murmured.

"You and me both."

A tall, pretty woman with a bit of gray in her short brown hair stepped forward. "You must be Princess Alexandra. I'm Cecilia, Mitch's mother. You can call me Cissy. Everyone does."

Alex dug deep for courage and poise she wasn't sure she had, then stepped free of Mitch's sheltering arms. She shook hands with both Mitch's parents. His father was a tall, handsome man who stood straight and had Mitch's teasing smile.

"So pleased to meet you," Alex said. "Have you met my parents?"

Her mother, Queen Gabriella, slipped her arm through Cissy's as if they'd known each other for years. "We've already had the pleasure, my dear. While you and Mitch were busy...talking."

"They're obviously right for each other," Cissy told Gabriella. "I knew it the minute I saw them together in that picture."

"I agree," the queen said. "I had about given up on her. I didn't think she was ever going to fall in love. Your Mitch seems like a very good man. He's done well with the ranch."

"Of course he has," Mitch's father said. "Taught him everything he knows."

"Robert, stop it," Cissy said, lightly touching her husband's arm.

King Phillip slapped Robert on the back. "I dare say you've hit the nail on the head. I've taken great pains to teach my children the right way and the wrong way. Any good father would, and I can see you've done well by your son. So, about the wedding."

Alex remembered watching a movie once in which the heroine was trapped behind a glass wall. She could talk or scream, but no one could hear her. That was how she felt this morning. Events were occurring around her, but she couldn't seem to participate.

"Yes," Cissy said, eyeing her son. "They seem to have handled things in reverse order, which I can almost guarantee was Mitch's fault."

Robert grinned. "That's because he's like his old man."

Cissy blushed. "Robert!"

Mitch groaned. "I did not want to know that."

"You think you two invented sex?" Robert asked testily. "I'll have you know that after thirty-five years your mother and I—"

"Robert!" This time Cissy's tone silenced her husband.

Gabriella gave the woman a knowing smile. "Phillip and I, as well. This is going to be a good match for our children. So let's talk about the wedding. What about something extravagant? Lots of flowers and guests. A sit-down dinner. I've always wanted to plan something like that when Alexandra finally married." She paused. "I would suggest Wynborough, except the staff is already taxed by the gala celebration next year."

"Then let's have it here," Robert said. "Plenty of room on the ranch. We don't have much time, though, with your Alex already being pregnant."

Alex flinched. This wasn't happening.

It was as if Mitch read her mind. He put a protective arm around her and raised his free hand. "That's it," he said. "While we appreciate all the advice, not to mention the planning, this isn't your decision to make."

King Phillip glared. "Are you sure you want to disagree with a king, young man? Not to mention your future father-in-law?"

"Not really, but I will anyway," Mitch told him evenly. "No one makes decisions about our future except us. As for who plans the wedding, how big it is and where it will be, or if there's going to be one, that's Alex's decision."

"Of course there will be a wedding," King Phillip told him.

"What's the problem?" Cissy asked. "You two love each other. You're going to have a baby together."

"What we're going to have is some privacy," Mitch said. He moved to the door. "I'm sure Betty has prepared coffee for the four of you. Please return to the living room and we'll join you as soon as we've figured everything out."

Everyone started backing out except King Phillip.

"Sir, this isn't your business," Mitch said respectfully, but firmly. "Alex and I will inform you of our decision when we've made it."

Her father glared, but Mitch didn't back down. Finally the older man took a step into the hall. "Thanks," Mitch said and closed the door.

Alex stared in disbelief as he shut out her father.

"You just slammed the door in a king's face," she said.

"I didn't slam it. I closed it firmly. This isn't about him, or anyone else. It's about us."

Alex looked at him. "You don't understand. No one stands up to the king. My father is a wonderful leader and is very willing to listen to all sides of a discussion, but he *is* the king. He never forgets that and neither do we."

"I didn't forget. But this isn't his decision to make." He stepped toward her, then pulled her close. "Now where were we?"

Alex thought about trying to explain the importance of what he'd just done, but she realized Mitch truly didn't care. If he thought King Phillip was getting in the way, he would tell the man. No doubt he would keep as close a watch on Alex, as well, making sure she didn't take on too many responsibilities, helping her stay balanced. He was even more wonderful than she'd known.

She slipped into his embrace. As his arms went around her, she felt as if she'd come home.

"I love you, Princess Alexandra," he said. "I haven't a clue as to how we're supposed to make this work, but I don't want to let you go. I want you to marry me." He smiled down at her. "And to answer the question before you ask it, I've been in love with you for a long time, but I didn't want to say anything. I wasn't sure I had very much to offer a woman like you."

"What changed your mind?" she asked, even though she knew the answer. It was her pregnancy.

She tried not to let that information make her sad. After all, many successful relationships had started with less.

"When I woke up this morning and you were gone," he said, "I knew no matter what, I couldn't spend my nights alone in that bed. I need you in my life. I'll do whatever it takes to allow us to be together."

She felt tears again, but this time tears of joy. "I love you, too, Mitch, and it's not about having a baby with you, although I'm very happy about that. It's because you're the best man I know. I would be proud to be your wife."

He kissed her hard, his tongue teasing hers, then he pulled back. "I'll never be a prince."

"You're wrong. You were born a prince. It's about character and strength, Mitch, not about titles. But I do have to warn you. My parents are going to insist that we attend the gala celebration in March in Wynborough."

"I can do that."

She couldn't help giggling. "That's not what I was warning you about. If I know my father, he's going to insist on knighting you."

Mitch groaned and rested his forehead against hers. "Do you know what the guys who work for me will say if they find that out? They'll make my life miserable."

"They'll just be jealous."

"You're right. Because I have you."

This time *she* kissed *him.* "We have a lot of things to work out."

"Uh-huh. I'll do what I have to to make you happy, but I want to insist on some time on the ranch each year." He reached out to caress her cheek.

"All right, but what about our parents?" she asked, even as she drew closer to him.

"Tell 'em whatever you want about the wedding. I don't care if there are fifty people there or fifty thousand. As long as you marry me."

"I meant that they're waiting for us in the living room."

He kissed her neck, then her cheeks, then her mouth. "They'd be thrilled if they knew."

She found herself laughing, then sighing as he cupped her face.

"I will love you forever, Princess Alexandra of Wynborough," he whispered, his mouth against hers.

Her heart swelled with joy at all that had happened to her. She'd come to this country searching for a brother. Instead she'd found the best man in the world. She knew they were going to have a wonderful life together.

"That's nearly as long as I'm going to love you," she promised.

* * * * *

Turn the page for a sneak preview
of the next magnificent
ROYALLY WED title

UNDERCOVER PRINCESS

Princess Katherine's story!

by bestselling author
Suzanne Brockmann,

on sale in November 1999
Silhouette Intimate Moments

Princess Katherine Wyndham drew in a deep breath. Here she was. Moments from meeting the man who could well help her answer all of her questions.

But how thrilled would he be to help her after he found out she'd used trickery and deceit to worm her way into his home? Of course, she'd been as tricked as he, but he couldn't know that. She'd better figure out what she was going to say, and she'd better do it quickly.

Katherine practiced her most winsomely royal smile. ''Mr. Sutherland. What a pleasure it is to finally meet you. But I do believe there's been something of a mix-up, sir. Your staff has mistaken me for the hired help, while in fact I am a princess. And that, sir, is why I've come to see you today. My elder brother, Prince James Wyndham, was abducted as an infant. He's been presumed dead these past nearly thirty years, but my three sisters and I have recently found reason to believe he may not have perished all those years ago. Mr. Sutherland, we believe that your elusive partner, one Mr. William Lewis, could in fact be our missing brother and the true heir to the Wynborough throne.''

Ah, yes.

That would go over quite excellently.

Katherine closed her eyes, imagining her sister Elizabeth and their social secretary, Laura Bishop, having to fly from Colorado to New Mexico to bale Katherine out of the lunatics' wing of the city jail.

This was a mistake—coming to Albuquerque this way. She wasn't cut out to play James Bond. That was much more Elizabeth's or Serena's speed.

But somehow something crazy had possessed Katherine. She'd agreed to come to Albuquerque, and now here she was.

Mistaken for a nanny.

Her fault completely.

She looked from the tightly closed doorway of Trey Sutherland's home office to the stairs that led back down to the front door.

Oh, dear.

As much as she wanted to, now that she was here, she simply couldn't walk away. If she were going to fail, it wasn't going to be from lack of trying.

She took another deep breath. ''Mr. Sutherland. What I have to say to you is going to sound *completely* insane, but I must ask you, sir, to—''

The door opened.

And there was Trey Sutherland.

Katherine had seen his picture. She had known he was outrageously handsome, but his photograph hadn't prepared her for the reality of the man.

He was taller than she'd expected—well over six feet. His shoulders took up nearly the entire doorway—shoulders clad in a dark gray business suit that looked as if it had been tailored to his exact measurements. His shirt was a lighter shade of that same gray, his collar unbuttoned, his tie rumpled and loose.

His hair was jet-black and messy, as if he'd been running his fingers through it in frustration. His face was harshly handsome, his mouth set in an expression of grimness. His eyes, although tired, redefined the color blue.

"Sorry to keep you waiting." His voice was a smooth baritone, without even a trace of a southwestern twang. "Come on in."

She had to move past him to enter his office. She went swiftly, aware of the subtle fragrance of his cologne, aware once again of his sheer size.

The phone on his desk rang, and Katherine froze, uncertain whether to go any farther or to retreat and wait, once again, out in the hall.

But Trey Sutherland closed his office door. "I'm sorry, I've got to take this. Why don't you sit down. I'll be right with you."

She gestured toward the door. "If you want, I don't mind…"

"No, this won't take long. Please. Sit."

As Katherine slowly perched on the edge of one of the leather armchairs positioned in front of Trey's rather lovely wooden desk, he picked up the telephone. He took the call standing behind his desk, his back to her as he gazed out the big picture window, his hand on his neck as if he were trying to loosen the tightly knotted muscles there.

''Sutherland.''

Moments later he turned to face her, making noises of agreement into the telephone and, while he thought she wasn't paying him any mind, sneaking a look at…her *legs?*

That was absurd. If anyone was going to dare to look at a princess's legs, he would look at Alexandra's or Elizabeth's legs, not Katherine's. While her legs weren't precisely unattractive, she simply didn't dress in a manner to draw a man's eyes in that direction. That is, assuming the man were bold enough to check out a princess in the first place. Most men weren't.

But, of course, Trey Sutherland had no idea Katherine was a princess. Trey Sutherland thought that Katherine was in his office to apply for a job as a nanny.

He hung up the phone. ''Sorry.''

''It's all right.''

In the brighter light of his office, she saw that there was a trace of silver at his temples. And his eyes really were a quite disarming shade of blue. His gaze swept over her again in a most disconcerting way. This time, it wasn't so much checking her out as assessing. Taking stock. Studying. There was nothing disrespectful about it—he was simply doing it in an extremely male way.

''Do you like kids?'' he said bluntly, coming

around to sit in the other leather armchair in front of his desk.

"Do I...?"

"Yeah, I know. It seems like a stupid question considering the job you're applying for, but I've run across more than my share of people claiming to be nannies who don't particularly like the children they've been hired to care for. They don't particularly like children at all." His eyes were hot with intensity as he leaned toward her. "My kids need to be respected and liked at the very least. And you better believe if I could pay you to love them, I would.

He stood up suddenly, as if he'd given too much away, or if there was a limit to how long he could contain his sheer energy and stay seated in a chair.

"My turn to apologize," he said, as he moved behind his desk. "Our last nanny left without even saying goodbye to Stacy and Doug. It's important to me that I find someone who fully understands the extent of the responsibility I'm placing upon them. These are kids who know too damn well what it means to be deserted, and— I'm getting way ahead of myself. I haven't even asked you your name."

"I do like kids," Katherine said softly. She liked kids, Trey Sutherland seemed in rather desperate need of a nanny, and if she kept up this insane subterfuge and moved into the Sutherland Estate, she'd be here when and if William Lewis turned up.

She'd also be here to watch Trey Sutherland's amazingly beautiful eyes blaze with intensity and passion. She imagined his eyes lit up that way at least several dozen times a day.

He smiled only very slightly, yet it was enough to soften the somewhat harsh lines of his face. "That's good to know, Miss...?

She tucked her hand behind her back, crossed her fingers, and for the first time in her life, acted on complete impulse.

"Wind," Princess Katherine of Wynborough said in her very best Sean Connery. "Kathy Wind."

Return to Whitehorn

Look for these bold new stories set in beloved Whitehorn, Montana!

CINDERELLA'S BIG SKY GROOM by Christine Rimmer
On sale October 1999 (Special Edition #1280)
A prim schoolteacher pretends an engagement
to the town's most confirmed bachelor!

A MONTANA MAVERICKS CHRISTMAS
On sale November 1999 (Special Edition #1286)
A two-in-one volume containing
two brand-new stories:

"Married in Whitehorn" by Susan Mallery
and
"Born in Whitehorn" by Karen Hughes

A FAMILY HOMECOMING by Laurie Paige
On sale December 1999 (Special Edition #1292)
A father returns home to guard his wife and child—
and finds his heart once more.

*Don't miss these books, only from
Silhouette Special Edition.*

Look for the next **MONTANA MAVERICKS** tale, by
Jackie Merritt, on sale in Special Edition May 2000.
And get ready for
MONTANA MAVERICKS: Wed in Whitehorn,
a new twelve-book series coming from Silhouette Books
on sale June 2000!

Available at your favorite retail outlet.

Silhouette®

Visit us at www.romance.net

SSEMAV

Silhouette® SPECIAL EDITION®

Don't miss the next poignant story coming to THAT'S MY BABY—only from Silhouette Special Edition!

December 1999
BABY BOY BLESSED by Arlene James (SE #1285)
Just as Lauren Cole seeks permanent custody of the precious infant left on her doorstep, a handsome stranger arrives with promises of passion—and a secret agenda—that could change her life forever....

THAT'S MY BABY!
Sometimes bringing up baby can bring surprises... and showers of love!

And for all of you fans of adorable babies, be sure to look for a brand-new four-book series:

SO MANY BABIES...

February 2000: THE BABY LEGACY by Pamela Toth
March 2000: WHO'S THAT BABY? by Diana Whitney
April 2000: MILLIONAIRE'S INSTANT BABY by Allison Leigh
May 2000: MAKE WAY FOR BABIES by Laurie Paige

Available at your favorite retail outlet.

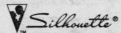

In December 1999
three spectacular authors invite you to share the
romance of the season as three special gifts are

Delivered by Christmas

A heartwarming holiday anthology featuring

BLUEBIRD WINTER
by *New York Times* bestselling author
Linda Howard

A baby is about to be born on the side of the road. The single
mother's only hope rests in the strong arms of a dashing doctor....

And two brand-new stories:

THE GIFT OF JOY
by national bestselling author **Joan Hohl**

A bride was not what a Texas-Ranger-turned-rancher was
expecting for the holidays. Will his quest for a home lead to love?

A CHRISTMAS TO TREASURE
by award-winning author **Sandra Steffen**

A daddy is all two children want for Christmas. And the
handsome man upstairs may be just the hero their mommy needs!

*Give yourself the gift of romance in
this special holiday collection!*

Available at your favorite retail outlet.

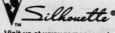

Visit us at www.romance.net

PSDBC